"There is a very big bed in there...."

"So?" Frankie asked when she hesitated.

"I suppose we could share it," Kelsey told him.

"It's okay with me," he said, giving her a wide grin. "Why don't you go in and change first? Then you can get under the covers."

"I'm going to sleep in a pair of shorts and a T-shirt," she responded, trying to sound blasé. "What do you sleep in?"

Frankie knew he was going to do it before he did it. He couldn't help himself. "I sleep in the buff. Just keep your eyes closed."

"What?" Kelsey wasn't absolutely certain he was teasing.

Frankie gave her a wink. "I have shorts with me."

Kelsey's heart was still beating quickly. "Outdoor shorts or boxer shorts?"

"Which do you prefer?"

Dear Reader,

This month, wedding bells ring for six couples who marry for convenient reasons—and discover love by surprise. Join us for their HASTY WEDDINGS.

Kasey Michaels starts off the month with *Timely Matrimony*, a love story with a time-travel twist. It's all in the timing for modern-day bride Suzi Harper, and Harry Wilde, her handsome husband from the nineteenth century. Just as they found happiness, it seemed Harry's destiny was to leave her....

In Anne Peters's *McCullough's Bride*, handsome rancher Nick McCullough rescues single mom Beth Coleman the only way he knows how—he marries her! Now Nick is the one in danger—of losing his heart to a woman who could never return his love.

Popular Desire author Cathie Linz weaves a *One of a Kind Marriage*. In this fast-paced romp, Jenny Benjamin and Rafe Murphy start as enemies, then become man and wife. Marriage may have solved their problems, but can love cure their differences?

The impromptu nuptials continue with *Oh, Baby!*, Lauryn Chandler's humorous look at a single woman who is determined to have a child—and lands herself a husband in the bargain. It's a green card marriage for Kelsey Shepherd and Frankie Falco in *Temporary Groom*. Jayne Addison continues her Falco Family series with this story of short-term commitment—and unending attraction! The laughter continues with Carolyn Zane's *Wife in Name Only*—a tale of marriage—under false pretenses.

I hope you enjoy our HASTY WEDDINGS. In the coming months, look for more books by your favorite authors.

Happy reading,

Anne Canadeo
Senior Editor

Please address questions and book requests to:
Silhouette Reader Service
U.S.: 3010 Walden Ave., P.O. Box 1325, Buffalo, NY 14269
Canadian: P.O. Box 609, Fort Erie, Ont. L2A 5X3

TEMPORARY GROOM

Jayne Addison

Silhouette
R O M A N C E™
Published by Silhouette Books
America's Publisher of Contemporary Romance

For Francis Fairclough,
my English daughter.

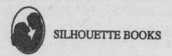 SILHOUETTE BOOKS

ISBN 0-373-19034-4

TEMPORARY GROOM

Copyright © 1994 by Jane Atkin

This edition published by arrangement with Harlequin Enterprises B. V.

® and TM are trademarks of Harlequin Enterprises B. V., used under license. Trademarks indicated with ® are registered in the United States Patent and Trademark Office, the Canadian Trade Marks Office and in other countries.

Printed in U.S.A.

Chapter One

"We are here this evening to join this man and this woman in the union of holy matrimony. Marriage is a time-honored institution and not to be taken lightly...."

Frankie suppressed an amused groan. There had to be over fifty wedding chapels along the strip; a number of them even had drive-through features. Getting married in Las Vegas was taken as lightly as buying fast food. They'd been in New York only this morning and one airplane ride later, here they were. They'd chose this chapel simply because it happened to be the one closest to their hotel. Frankie bet it wasn't the only one with an Elvis Presley imitator ministering out vows.

"Do you, Kelsey Shepherd, take Frank Falco to be your lawfully wedded husband, to have and to hold in sickness and in health, to honor and comfort in sorrow and joy, to cherish until death do you part?''

This wasn't the kind of wedding she'd anticipated back in London. This wasn't even the man she'd anticipated marrying. Kelsey had met the man standing next to her only three days ago—and she was including today. He'd been wearing a black T-shirt with some slogan written across it when she'd first seen him. It might have read Loose And Easy, but that could have been just something she'd thought because of his attitude. He was good-looking: lean, wiry, slim hipped and not too muscular. But his dark hair, dark eyes, straight nose and strong chin had nothing at all to do with this marriage ceremony. This was all the idea of Charlie Peterson, her American grandfather. He'd introduced them. He'd come up with this brainstorm.

Kelsey swallowed. How could she have agreed to marry a total stranger in order to get herself a green card? All she really knew about Frankie Falco was that he had as much to gain out of this marriage as she did.

Was it legal to be married by an Elvis Presley impersonator?

"Miss Shepherd?" The minister, who, aside from the costume and fake sideburns, looked nothing at all like the real Elvis Presley, pitched his upper body forward. "Did you hear the question?"

Kelsey leaned back to get "Elvis" out of her space. She didn't feel all that great.

Frankie flashed a glance at Kelsey, and quickly spoke to the minister. "Could we have a moment, please?"

"Elvis" looked over to an older woman who was standing to the side. "Well, Mama, think we can give these folks a moment?"

Kelsey turned her face just enough to bring "Mama" into focus. It was an awkward maneuver given she was light-headed.

Mama, amply figured in a bold flowered dress, wasn't emoting pleasure at the prospect of an intermission.

"We can't hold the ceremony up for long," the older woman said censoriously. "There are a lot of couples waiting to take their vows. We have a schedule to run."

With Frankie's hand on her forearm prodding her, Kelsey marched backward with him, taking three giant steps out from under the arched trellis, which was decorated with artificial flowers and dusty papier-mâché doves.

"Do you want to call this off?" Frankie asked in an undertone.

"Do you?" Kelsey experienced palpable relief at the prospect.

"It's your call," Frankie responded. He'd thought that they'd both agreed this arrangement made sense after their initial shock at Charlie's proposal had worn off. Personally, he always stuck with a decision once he made one, even though, more often than not, his choice was the wrong one.

"You interrupted the proceedings." Kelsey threw the ball right back. She didn't want to be the one to call it quits. She didn't want to spend the rest of her life thinking she'd backed away from her one big chance. She might never get such an opportunity again.

"I interrupted because I thought you were about to faint," Frankie replied. He noticed that she seemed a little less pale now.

"I don't faint." Unconsciously, Kelsey tucked her curvy cognac-brown hair behind her ears, trying to cool herself regardless of the fact that the air-conditioning was blowing full blast.

Frankie kneaded the back of his neck. "I hate to tell you this, but you've lost one of your earrings." He hadn't been aware that she was even wearing any when her hair had fallen over her ears to her shoulders. The one earring she still had on was gold with two dangling copper beads that almost matched the color of her eyes, except that her eyes were vividly brighter. The first thing he had noticed about her had been her eyes.

"I haven't lost an earring," she replied, moving her hair forward. "I only wear one."

"Why?" He asked the obvious.

Kelsey ignored his question and brought the conversation back to the topic of their impending marriage. "Maybe we should talk this through some more."

Frankie let out a breath. "We've talked this thing inside, outside, sideways and front."

Kelsey drew in a breath. "We talked about the scheme. We plotted out the details. We came up with a plausible story. What we didn't talk about is what happens after this ceremony. This really ridiculous ceremony."

Frankie stuck his hands into the pockets of his front-pleated grayish blue slacks, bunching up his navy blazer. "Afterward, we just follow the scheme."

Kelsey gave him an exasperated look. This wasn't like deciding whether to have eggs with or without kippers for breakfast. "What if we can't get along? You don't know what I'm like. I don't know what you're like. And we're going to be living together.... I think Charlie would still offer you the loan even if you don't go through with this wedding. You can buy your partner out and redo your pub."

"Bar and grill," Frankie corrected. "Even if your grandfather is willing, I'm not willing to accept any loan from him unless I can give him what he wants. And he wants you to be able to stay in New York."

Kelsey chewed the side of her mouth.

Frankie blew out another breath. "What about your green card? Don't you still want that job you've been offered? You've been going on and on about it."

"I want it." *Style Magazine*—staff fashion photographer for *Style Magazine*. It was the dream job of a lifetime. Her career hadn't been going anywhere in London.

"Do you want to spend the rest of your life asking yourself 'What if?'"

She could have done without him verbalizing that "what if" question. "Let's just do it!" she practically yelled.

Frankie gestured with both his hands for her to precede him. "Anytime you're ready." He probably wasn't going to like her. She was most likely a classic type A personality.

Walking as if her feet were stuck in cement, Kelsey moved forward. She wasn't going to like him. She could tell that already.

"Do you need me to repeat the question?" "Elvis" asked, not very politely, when Kelsey and Frankie were in place.

"I do," Kelsey gulped. "No, I mean no."

"Are you going to marry this guy?" "Elvis" inquired, no longer looking as if he might break into a love ballad.

Frankie held his breath.

"Yes," Kelsey rasped.

"Elvis" needlessly adjusted the scarf around his neck. "Do you, Frank Falco, take Kelsey Shepherd to be your wedded wife, to have and to hold in sickness and in health, to honor and comfort in sorrow and in joy, to cherish until death do you part?"

"I do." *Just till she gets her green card.* Frankie nodded.

"Do you have the ring?"

Frankie put his hand into the pocket of his blazer and pulled out a ten-dollar gold-plated band.

"Frank, please put the ring on Kelsey's finger and repeat after me."

Frankie took hold of Kelsey's left hand. It was limp.

"You might want to look at each other so Mama can take a picture," "Elvis" suggested thinly.

Kelsey and Frankie each gave a stiff half shift. Kelsey focused on the knot of his navy blue tie. She had no idea where he was looking.

"Elvis" reached out and tilted Kelsey's chin up. The flash went off. Kelsey brought her chin back down.

"Frank, now repeat after me. With this ring I thee wed."

"With this ring I thee wed." Frankie wasn't positive, but he thought he'd heard an Elvis-like twang coming out of his own mouth. The ring went on easily, as it was slightly big for her.

"By the power vested in me by the state of Nevada, I now pronounce you husband and wife. You may kiss the bride." The two sentences ran into each other. "Elvis" had spoken them rapidly.

Kelsey gazed heavenward and caught a view of the red velvet-covered ceiling of the Love Me Tender chapel. There was a tear in the cloth.

Frankie paused and, without attempting to embrace her, planted a quick kiss between her chin and her nose. He figured he'd landed somewhere in the vicinity of her mouth.

"Elvis" quickly signed their wedding certificate and extended it to Frankie along with the instant photo Mama had taken.

Frankie folded the wedding certificate and stuck it, along with the photo, in the inside pocket of his jacket. He might have given up his freedom for a while—so to speak—but he didn't feel as if he'd lost his sense of humor. This wedding scene would have made a great skit for a comedy show.

"Well, I guess that's it," Kelsey said, and breathed in and out just to make sure she still knew how. She could feel perspiration on her forehead. What had she gotten herself into?

Frankie quirked Kelsey a grin. "I guess so."

Kelsey didn't know what she'd anticipated from him, but it hadn't been amusement.

"What?" Frankie asked, responding to her expression.

"Nothing." Kelsey flicked her palms in the air before she walked up the aisle on rubbery legs.

Frankie didn't move to her side. He stayed behind her, keeping his hands ready to catch her if she went down.

Once outside, Kelsey took several deep breaths of the humid night air.

Frankie could see her clearly in the overabundance of neon lights all around. Some color had returned to her face. "How about I get a cab to take us back to the hotel?"

"That's silly," Kelsey said as she began walking. The hotel was in easy walking distance.

"Would you like to go for something to eat?" She was Charlie's granddaughter, after all, Frankie thought. It wouldn't kill him to be civil to her.

"I'm not hungry, but thank you for asking." How could he even think about eating? She was in a total turmoil. She didn't know if she could ever eat again.

"How about a drink?" He figured they could both use one.

Kelsey's eyes moved to Frankie's face. She took in his wavy dark hair and brown eyes, which even if he wasn't trying for the effect, were blatantly sexy. "I think I'll just make it an early night." She didn't see the need for them to socialize just because they'd gotten married.

"Immigration might decide to check out what kind of honeymoon we've had. Maybe we should see if we can get our picture taken at some club? You can bring your camera along."

Kelsey blanched. "I didn't think about that when we registered for separate rooms."

Frankie shrugged gamely. He hadn't been thinking about their room situation, either. It did deserve some consideration. "We can fix it. We'll see if they have a suite. That will give us each a room to sleep in."

"If immigration does check, how will we explain why we took separate rooms at first?" Kelsey's mind was flying ahead of itself, considering the worst. They'd hardly gotten started and they'd already blundered. It was a bad sign.

"We weren't married when we registered," Frankie answered, thinking quickly.

"I guess that makes sense." Kelsey walked faster.

Frankie easily matched her stride. Within minutes they reached the hotel.

The double metallic doors to Chesaro's Palace slid open automatically. Frankie allowed Kelsey to precede him into the lobby. He'd selected the hotel, having been to Vegas before. Chesaro's was considerably less expensive than the larger, more glittery hotels on the strip. She'd made it clear she wasn't looking to splurge, since they were splitting expenses.

The casino, just to the side of the lobby, was wall-to-wall people, all noisily trying to fulfill their fantasies at gaming tables and slot machines. It had been just as busy in the casino when Kelsey and Frankie had first arrived, and when they'd left to go over to the chapel.

Kelsey and Frankie headed straight for the front desk.

"Do you happen to have a honeymoon suite?" Frankie asked the man behind the counter. He was thirtyish, big and wide through the shoulders. He probably doubled as a bouncer.

"Sure, but aren't you already checked in?"

"Right, but we just got married." With characteristic insouciance, Frankie draped his arm around Kelsey's shoulders. Taking a cue from the pointed directive Frankie was giving her with his eyes, Kelsey manufactured a dopey smile as she gazed up at her new husband. He was easily a foot taller than she, and she was fairly tall.

"I can switch you to a suite," the man behind the counter told them. "I'll send a bellboy up to your rooms. You'll have to reregister first."

With Kelsey looking over his shoulder, Frankie signed the register slip. Mr. and Mrs. Frank Falco. Kelsey read the words, but she still couldn't believe they'd actually done the deed.

Frankie took out his wallet from the inside pocket of his jacket to pay the additional charge after being credited for their two rooms. He was fairly certain that he was being stiffed. But what the hell.... Love was supposed to be blind.

"I'll give you my share for the additional cost," Kelsey said as they crossed the lobby to the bank of elevators opposite the casino.

Frankie nodded indifferently. She'd made this particular point more times than he needed to hear. Breakfast this morning and lunch had been dutch, not that she'd eaten very much. He figured that she didn't want to feel beholden to him in any way.

One of the heavily scrolled elevator doors opened. Kelsey and Frankie waited for it to empty of animated diners and gamblers before stepping in. They were alone on the elevator.

"Did you unpack?" Frankie asked conversationally as he pressed the button for the tenth floor.

"No." Kelsey took her room key from the small beige clutch bag she was carrying. "I just pulled this dress out to change into." Her dress was a floral print on a cream background. It was a simple style—cap-sleeve bodice, high Empire waist, long shirred skirt and pearlized buttons from neck to hem. A bit artsy, perhaps. Not at all the kind of dress she'd expected to wear to her wedding.

Frankie scanned her from head to toe—not that he hadn't already taken notice of her appearance. He did like the dress on her. He hadn't seen her in anything but jeans until this evening. She looked equally good in jeans. Actually, she'd looked better than good in jeans.

The elevator opened on their floor without having made any stops. Kelsey and Frankie walked through the open doors, into the hallway. They moved a short distance to their rooms, which were side-by-side.

"Well," Kelsey said uncomfortably at her door. She found it extremely unsettling that he didn't seem even the least bit rattled.

"Well." Frankie gave her a quick smile. "See you in a few minutes."

Kelsey put the key in her lock, turned the knob and walked in. She closed the door behind her, fell back against it and tried to calm down. She was all shook-up.

* * *

The bellhop, a young man with a serious crew cut, and carrying himself as if he was in military service, walked them to their suite. It was just down the hall from their previous rooms. Kelsey and Frankie remained standing in the sitting room while the bellhop deposited each of their suitcases in the second room to the suite. Kelsey was not ready to inspect the bedroom. Instead, she stood where she was and looked around.

Frankie placed his attention on the upholstered furniture. He'd anticipated a couch, but found the room contained only two love seats, plus a couple of chairs. Frankie could already feel a crick in his neck, his back and his knees.

"Do you want a Do Not Disturb sign on the knob?" the bellhop asked with a meaningful look as he stopped at the front door.

"Sounds like a plan," Frankie said with a smile, taking his wallet out of his pocket.

"Thank you, sir," the bellhop responded after being tipped. He closed the door behind him.

There was no avoiding the moment. From opposite ends of the room Kelsey and Frankie assessed each other. She wasn't thinking of asking how much the tip had been so she could offer her half. That didn't even come to her mind. Her thoughts were centered on the Do Not Disturb sign that was hanging outside the door.

Frankie could see that she was now even more uptight. He was a little jumpy himself. He started toward her, trying to think of something to say to break the ice.

Kelsey moved to the side, crisscrossing his approach. "There's a small kitchen." It was only a few steps away from where she'd started. It didn't take her long to get there—just a turn around the counter and bar stools.

Frankie headed over to join her.

"There's a coffeemaker," Kelsey said, hearing herself sound as if she'd just discovered a pot of gold. "Oh, and they've left us coffee." She bent to open the door to a small refrigerator under the counter. She didn't even drink coffee.

Frankie loosened the knot of his tie and unbuttoned the collar of his light blue shirt. He sat on one of the stools, and peered down over the counter at her.

"This is just a wild guess, but is something bothering you?"

"No," Kelsey answered, her face buried in the refrigerator.

Frankie tapped a rhythm with his fingers on the countertop. "Did I make you uncomfortable because I told the bellboy to put on the Do Not Disturb sign?"

Kelsey gave him a quick glance, then returned her gaze to the refrigerator. "Don't be ridiculous."

"Believe me, you don't have to be nervous. I'm tapped into my best behavior. I just said it because it was clearly expected." He couldn't imagine there was enough in the refrigerator to keep her as engrossed as she seemed to be.

Kelsey's eyes shot back to Frankie's face. "I'm not nervous."

Frankie cocked his head. "You seem nervous."

"I just don't know what to do with myself." She didn't want to look into the refrigerator anymore. All there was in there were six small bottles of club soda and a few minipackaged snacks.

"Dinner and drinks are still open."

Kelsey closed the refrigerator and straightened. "I guess you're starving."

Frankie braced his elbow on the counter. "Actually, I'm not all that hungry. I'm just nervous like you."

"You are?" Kelsey studied him more closely. He was certainly good at covering it.

"Uh-huh." Frankie held her gaze. She did have exceptional eyes—not that there was anything wrong with the rest of her features.

"Oh..." Kelsey broke eye contact without deciding if he actually was discomforted. He had just discomforted her even more. "Should we call Charlie?"

Frankie lifted his shirt cuff to check his watch. "He's probably cooking up a storm about now.... I hope he's cooking up a storm. Anyway, he'll know we went through with it if he doesn't hear from us. I promised I'd call if we changed our minds."

"How long have you known Charlie?" Normal conversation. That's what she needed.

"I bought into the bar just about a year ago. Your grandfather was already one of the fixtures there. He's a terrific cook."

"You like each other a lot." It was more of a statement than a question. She'd seen that for herself.

"Yes." Frankie included a smile with his reply.

Kelsey turned her head aslant. "Could I ask you a personal question?" She hadn't realized before, but the way his mouth angled more to one side when he smiled was as sexy as the glint of his eyes.

Frankie teasingly raised an eyebrow. He didn't see that some bantering could hurt. "I think as my wife you're entitled to at least one."

"How's your girlfriend taking this?" Kelsey hoped she didn't sound as if she were prying, but she was curious.

Frankie shrugged carelessly. "She's okay with it." He didn't want to tell her that he and Monica had broken up, and have Kelsey tell Charlie. He wasn't going to stick Charlie with an unnecessary guilt trip. The truth of the matter was that this imitation marriage had only been a catalyst. The relationship had become routine for both of them, without them knowing it. This situation brought that to light. It was just as well. He had a business he intended to give his full attention to. It was high time he made something of himself.

"Really?" Kelsey gave Frankie a look from the corner of her eye.

"It isn't anything that I can't work out."

She'd been so preoccupied with her own problems, Kelsey realized she hadn't given his dilemma any thought until now. "Maybe I should go see her. I could reassure her that this is strictly an arrangement."

Stretching, Frankie flexed his shoulder muscles. "I don't think seeing you will reassure her."

A startled expression came over Kelsey's face. "Is that a compliment?" A come-on was more the inference her mind was making.

Frankie considered his meaning for a second. "I guess it is."

"I don't think you should be complimenting me," Kelsey stated firmly.

"Why not?"

"You have a girlfriend," Kelsey expostulated.

"So?" He studied her with perplexity.

Handing him a look of utter incredulity, Kelsey walked around the counter, back into the sitting area. Was this an example of his best behavior? He hadn't tapped very deeply into that well.

Frankie swiveled around on his bar stool and watched as she sat on one of the gold brocade love seats. Smoothing her dress down over her legs, she said, "I certainly hope that we will act friendly toward each other...."

"But not too friendly," Frankie cut in. He knew the punch line.

"Exactly," Kelsey confirmed.

There was a pause during which Kelsey fidgeted and Frankie observed her.

"I hope you understand that I wasn't accusing you of flirting with me," Kelsey said, backing down after having reconsidered for a second. There was a chance she might have been mistaken.

He had been flirting with her a little, Frankie realized, though he didn't consider it to be a big deal. "With what you've been through, I can understand how you'd be a little defensive right now."

"I am not defensive," Kelsey replied defensively. "I may have just come out of a difficult situation, but I'm handling it well. At least, I think so, anyway."

He knew her story. She'd met a guy from New York while he was in London on business six months ago. The guy had romanced her and she'd fallen for him. She'd come to New York expecting to marry him. Only he'd neglected to mention that he happened to be already married.

"Okay." He didn't think that she had it together yet.

"Okay to what?" Kelsey asked, irked. She decided that Frankie Falco's personality could be very annoying.

"Okay to whatever we're arguing about." Frankie gave her his infamous smile, trying to joke with her.

"I'm not arguing," Kelsey responded combatively.

Frankie figured this might be a good time for him to take a turn at looking inside the refrigerator. At the very least, he decided to keep his mouth shut for a while.

There was a long silence.

Finally, Frankie took a stab at conversation. "We should be really proud of ourselves that we're getting along at all."

"You're doing better than I am." Kelsey didn't like having to concede, but it was quite evident.

"I wouldn't say that." *Not out loud, anyway.*

"It's the truth," Kelsey replied. "Maybe I am a little defensive."

Frankie got up from the stool and went over to sit next to her. "There isn't anything wrong with being a little defensive. Do you want to talk about it?"

"No." Kelsey sighed heavily. "Do you know what I hate?"

"What do you hate?" Frankie encouraged.

"That he thought I'd actually want to continue our relationship. He even expected me to believe that he's thinking of getting a divorce. I should have been suspicious that he never gave me his home address to write to him, that and the fact that he always called me. He said he didn't want me to spend my money calling him. I guess he just wanted to keep me on the string in London for his next business trip."

Frankie didn't know what to say to try to make her feel better. The guy was a first-class bum.

"The women in my family don't seem to have any luck with men. My grandmother and Charlie were divorced. Did Charlie tell you that they met when he was stationed in London?"

Frankie nodded, but she turned her head just then so he answered, "Yes."

"They got married because my grandmother was pregnant. They got divorced just a few months after my mother was born. Divorce runs in my family. My mother and father got divorced when I was ten. Now here I am doing exactly what I promised myself I'd never do. I'm planning my own divorce." Kelsey raised one hand haplessly.

Frankie put his hand to her chin and brought her face around. "How about we enjoy our one-night honeymoon first? As soon as the words were out of his mouth Frankie realized how they must have sounded to her, especially given the eloquent emotion that had quickly come into her eyes. He rushed to explain. "That was a slip of the tongue... a bad slip of the tongue. What I meant was how about we go down to the casino and see how long it takes to lose a hundred bucks? My hundred bucks. It's my idea." He gave her what he hoped was an irresistibly coaxing look.

"Only if we make it fifty dollars each." She didn't really want to spend the evening alone. And perhaps his personality wasn't all that annoying.

Frankie gave her his sexiest smile.

Chapter Two

It was two in the morning when Kelsey and Frankie returned to their hotel suite. Kelsey placed her camera down carefully on a side table, then flopped onto one of the love seats. She was exhausted, but too exhilarated to sleep. "That hotel with the white tigers and volcanoes was unbelievable!"

Frankie nodded and gave her a smile. He was seated across from her on the other love seat, his legs stretched out under the coffee table between them. "Did you really win at the slot machines?" he asked, bantering with her. He was certain she'd walked away clean.

"Did you really win shooting those dice?" Kelsey bantered back at him. She'd lost the fifty dollars she'd allotted herself for gambling, as well as an additional ten dollars.

"I've never shot that many points in my life," Frankie proclaimed dramatically. He'd lost seventy-five bucks. "I wanted to teach you how to shoot craps, but you said no."

"Maybe I should have taken a break from winning. I think I may have pulled my arm out of its socket." Kelsey rotated her shoulder."

"You have to watch those one-arm bandits. They're addictive." Frankie watched Kelsey pull her shoulders back and forward and pinch them together. She was small-breasted, but the exercise she was doing drew his gaze to the front of her dress.

"There was a woman next to me who must have lost about five hundred quarters," Kelsey remarked.

Frankie got up and prowled around. "Is it hot in here?" he asked. "Or is it just me?"

"I'm fine," Kelsey answered blithely. "You can turn the air conditioner up higher if you want."

Frankie took off his jacket and tossed it onto one of the armchairs. He pulled open his tie and dropped it on top of his jacket. Then he opened the top two buttons of his shirt. He knew what his agitation was all about. It had to do with the power of suggestive reasoning. He had a case of honeymoonitis.

It was a few moments before Kelsey became aware of the quiet. She'd been caught up thinking about the photos she'd taken.

Kelsey was surprised to notice that Frankie's hair was all tousled. She hadn't been aware that he'd combed it with his fingers a dozen or so times. She also noticed that he'd undressed a bit—she could see that he had on a white T-shirt under his dress shirt. "Are you tired?" she asked him.

"No." Frankie shook her head. "Are you tired?"

"No, but we should work out our sleeping arrangement. I insist you take the bedroom." Kelsey pictured the king-size bed. She'd caught sight of it when she'd gone through the bedroom on the way to the bathroom before they'd left for their night on the town.

He thought her offer was sweet. "I can do just fine on the floor in here. All I need is a pillow, and I'll take the spread off the bed."

"That doesn't make sense. I can curl up on one of these love seats."

"Would you like something from room service?" Frankie asked, wanting to change the subject before it fed his agitation.

"Yes." Kelsey nodded. "I'd love some tea."

"How about something to go with it?" Frankie sat back down opposite her.

"No." Kelsey shook her head. "Do you think they could send up a whole pot of tea?"

"Sure." Frankie picked up the phone from the nearby side table and called room service. He ordered a pot of tea, and a beer for himself.

As soon as Frankie hung up, Kelsey started to speak. Frankie began to say something in the same instant. They overlapped each other, then stopped before either had completed a sentence.

"You first," Kelsey said, waving her hand at him.

"No, you first." Frankie pointed a finger at her.

"Really...I insist." She couldn't remember what it was she'd been about to say. She had only been trying to get a conversation started.

He'd been about to ask if her shoulder felt any better. Now that he contemplated it, he didn't want to stimulate any more shoulder movement on her part.

"I was just going to ask about the magazine you're planning to work for." He pulled that thought out of thin air.

Kelsey liked the topic. "It's a new magazine. They're just starting up. They won't be into production for a couple of months. I sent them an inquiry and a sampling of my work when I read about them in a trade publication. I can still hardly believe they've accepted me. I've only been able to manage free-lance work at home, and that's hardly been steady.

"Do they know you don't have a green card?" Frankie questioned when Kelsey paused.

"I told them I was going to be able to get one." Kelsey raised her hand and showed Frankie she had her fingers crossed. "Meanwhile, I have a two-month visa. Hopefully I'll have the card before they call me to start working."

There was a knock on the door. Kelsey and Frankie both got to their feet. "I know I'm behind in my share," Kelsey said, grabbing her handbag. "Let me pay."

Frankie negated her offer. "I'm just going to sign for it. We'll straighten it out tomorrow when we leave."

Kelsey sat back down while Frankie went to the door, letting in the bellhop who had seen them to their suite earlier.

"Where would you like this?" the young man asked, a tray with their order in hand.

"On the cocktail table." Frankie motioned, then followed him over.

"Thank you, sir." The bellhop acknowledged the additional twenty percent Frankie had added when he signed for the order. The young man quickly saw himself out.

Kelsey noted that the kitchen had thoughtfully sent up sugar, cream and lemon, giving her a range of choices. She poured herself a cup of tea, adding a splash of cream. She was pleased to see that the tea was well brewed. She'd wanted it to be strong.

Frankie flipped the cap off the beer bottle with his thumb. He took a swallow, not bothering with the frosted mug on the tray. "I just realized that I don't even know how old you are." He was watching her sip. There was a tiny dimple at the corner of her mouth that hadn't registered on him until now.

"Twenty-seven. I'll be twenty-eight in three months. The twelfth of September." She wondered what his girlfriend looked like. "How old are you?" She put down her cup.

"Thirty. I'll be thirty-one in December." He eyed the way she was toying with her hair. "You never did tell me why you only wear one earring."

"It's just a personal theory of mine." Kelsey did recall that she'd babbled an earful of her personal history earlier.

"What if someone at immigration asks me why you only wear one earring?" Frankie's eyes held laughter while he improvised his next words. "You might not like the story I'd make up and how would you know my story when they asked you? A little thing like an earring could trip us up."

Kelsey didn't particularly think that a matter such as one earring was going to come up with immigration, but she didn't want Frankie speculating on the subject without knowing what reason he had conjured up. "It's to remind me that I'm looking for my heart."

Frankie grinned broadly. "I never took anatomy, but I think I could draw you an *X*."

"I'm speaking symbolically," Kelsey said in mock reprimand.

Frankie affected a studious expression. "What do you mean by symbolically?"

Kelsey tipped her head to one side. "This very important art critic told me once, and not very kindly, that if I ever want my photography to really say something I was going to have to shoot my pictures less with my mind and more with my heart. From what he saw of my work, I hadn't found my heart. I manage technically, but I'm too structured. I've decided that wearing only one earring might remind me not to be so structured. This probably sounds dumb...."

Frankie shook his head. "How will you know when you've found your heart?" He was bemused and engaged by her explanation.

"That's the tricky part." Kelsey lifted one shoulder and let it drop. "I haven't any idea how I'll know."

"What did you mean when you said you were too structured?"

Without conscious thought, Kelsey twirled her hair again. "I guess what I mean is that I rarely go with my instincts, and I don't mean just as a photographer. I spend too much time thinking about whether I should or shouldn't."

Frankie interjected. "You might be doing yourself a favor by taking time out to think." More often than not, Frankie knew he would have done himself a favor if he'd taken time out to think instead of jumping on just about every impulse he'd ever had. He hoped that taking over the bar was going to tip the scale. It was about time he found himself and stopped being a lousy bet.

Kelsey drank some more of her tea. "I'd like to be more daring, instead of always trying to plan every step of the way."

"I've been bouncing around my entire adult life without a plan." Frankie rolled his bottle of beer between his two hands. "It hasn't gotten me very far." He'd bought into the bar with Billy DeSilva because he'd gotten bored selling used cars. He'd had a couple of bucks. Billy had had an equal amount, and the owner of the place had been willing to hold a note for the rest.

"You have a plan now," Kelsey amplified. "You're going to buy your partner out and refurbish the place."

It hadn't come as a big shock to him when Billy had decided he wanted out. Billy didn't stick with anything any longer than he himself usually did.

"How about we toast to my plan and your dream job?" Frankie raised his beer bottle.

Kelsey lifted her cup of tea. "To helping each other out."

Frankie smiled and said, "The dream team," while he tapped his bottle to her cup.

Kelsey sipped her tea. Frankie drank some beer. Their gazes drifted over each other.

Looking for a distraction, Kelsey poured herself a refill. Her stomach was fluttery, which made no sense to her at all. She'd eaten a full dinner.

"Don't you think you've been more than a little daring by marrying me?" Frankie asked, a teasing expression on his face.

Kelsey digested that thought and gave Frankie a plucky smile. "Charlie can be bullheaded."

He wondered what she'd look like right after a shower with her hair damp and with the little makeup she used on her face gone.

"Did I understand right that the first time you even met your grandfather was eight months ago when you came to New York on vacation?" He tried to decide half-seriously which was more intoxicating, his third beer for the night, or her eyes.

Kelsey nodded.

Frankie took a swig from his beer bottle. "What does your mother have against your grandfather?"

"How do you know my mother has anything against Charlie?" Kelsey felt herself instantly exchanging the sense of rapport she'd been establishing with him for a need to be defensive. The subject he'd just brought up was complicated and touchy for her.

"Your grandfather told me." Frankie tossed back another gulp of beer. He could see that she wanted to designate any questions regarding her relationship with her grandfather as off-limits. It was written on her face.

"I don't suppose that Charlie mentioned that after my mother was born he decided he just wasn't into responsibility?" She wasn't looking to cast any aspersions on the high esteem he held Charlie Peterson in.

The censure in her question was out of her mouth before she'd thought it through.

"He mentioned something to that effect. He said he was very young. He hadn't been ready for marriage, let alone becoming a father." Frankie knew he shouldn't be pushing his way into her family matters, but he found himself barging ahead anyway.

"My grandmother was just as young as Charlie when he walked out leaving her with a baby to take care of." This wasn't a conversation she wanted to be having, but since he'd gotten her into it, Kelsey intended to get her point across.

"Charlie did finally straighten himself out and send your grandmother money for your mother's support. He never stopped sending money, though your grandmother refused to allow him any visits."

"I think my grandmother was right not to allow him to visit. My mother feels that Charlie should have put up more of a fight to be something of a father to her. Now she's not interested in knowing him at all."

"If you feel so negative about your grandfather, what made you decide to look him up eight months ago?"

"I was curious about him."

"Do you know that your grandfather has worked two jobs most of his life so he could put away an inheritance to leave your mother?" He thought that was something she should know.

"My mother has done fine for herself. She doesn't need an inheritance."

"He's putting it up now to keep you around."

"It's his money." Kelsey shrugged. Charlie working two jobs most of his life to save an inheritance for her mother wasn't something she'd cared to know about.

"You talk tough, but I don't think you're anywhere near as tough as you try to sound."

"You're entitled to your opinion."

"It's got to be rough doing the balancing act you're doing between your mother and grandfather. I've noticed that every time you seem to start to warm up to him, you pull back and act cool."

"Maybe I'm just naturally cool."

Frank brought his bottle of beer to his mouth and swallowed. "Do you want to change the subject?"

Kelsey took a drink of her tea and changed the subject. "My mother is going to be shocked when I tell her that I'm married—but not to Eric."

"Are you going to tell your mother that our getting married is just an arrangement?"

"No." Kelsey decided that answer on the spot. "She wouldn't like the idea, especially knowing that Charlie is involved. It will be easier for her to think that it turned out that we just weren't compatible."

He wondered if she was thinking about the history of the females in her family that she'd told him about earlier. He didn't feel it was good for her to be thinking that way.

"If you're not going to tell your mother the truth, what are you going to tell her?" He wouldn't have been surprised if she was hoping deep down that one day her mother and her grandfather would patch up their differences.

"I'll tell my mother the story we're going to give immigration—that we met when I was here eight months ago and that we corresponded between then and now."

"How will you fit Eric into that scenario?" He hadn't known the name of the bum she'd gotten caught up with until she'd just mentioned it.

"I'll just say Eric was a fling. That I hadn't realized I'd been falling in love with you through your letters. When I saw you again, I knew you were the one for me."

Frankie thought about throwing out a sexy remark, but he didn't. He did get antsy again—the same kind of antsiness he'd felt when he had been pacing around.

Kelsey watched Frankie take another drink from his bottle of beer. She wondered how he'd photograph. He was as virile as any male model she'd ever met. She could see him in an Italian menswear ad in *GQ*. "What are you going to tell your family?"

Frankie rubbed the neck of the bottle across his lower lip. Then he lowered it and smiled. "I think I'll just tell them that I got hit by the Italian thunderbolt."

Kelsey didn't get it. "What does that mean?"

"The Italian thunderbolt is kind of a Cupid's arrow, but with an even sharper point."

Kelsey rolled her eyes. "But what about me? Am I supposed to have been hit by the thunderbolt, too, and wouldn't I have to be Italian to feel it?"

Frankie winked. "It's the Italian male that the thunderbolt goes after. You wouldn't have been able to fight me off once I'd taken the hit."

"Your family is actually going to accept this idea?" She was pretty certain that he was putting her on.

"You'll be able to see for yourself. You're going to be with me when I tell them." He did plan to give his family the same story she was going to give her mother—they same story they were going to relate to immigration. He'd done some wild things in his life, but all that was minor league compared to now. This was one wild thing he was going to keep to himself.

Kelsey's eyes seemed to double in size. "No, I'm not!"

"Didn't you promise to stick by my side for better or worse?"

"I didn't hear anything about 'and be there when he tells his family,'" Kelsey countered impudently. She had the feeling that she was flirting with him, but she was too tired to give it a lot of thought.

Frankie smiled slowly. "It's written right in the wedding certificate . . . the fine print on the bottom."

"Really, what are you going to tell your family?"

Frankie lounged on the love seat. "Are you saying that you don't believe that there is an Italian thunderbolt?" He liked her responses to his ribbing.

"Is there a book on the subject?" Kelsey countered.

Frankie grinned. "My brother, Teddy, got hit with the Italian thunderbolt. He married my sister-in-law after knowing her less than ten days. There wasn't anyone in the family who had any trouble accepting their romance."

Kelsey didn't know where else to go with this conversation. "All right. Fine."

"You'd better be prepared—my mother and father are going to want to throw us a party like they did for Teddy and Quinn."

"Tell me about your family," Kelsey requested, hoping to turn the conversation to a more serious topic.

"I have four siblings. Nancy is the oldest. She's married to Shep. They have twin daughters. Then there's Angie. Rick, Angie's first husband, died in the line of duty. He was a police officer. They had two daughters together. A year or so after Rick was killed, Angie married Rick's brother, Sonny. Angie fought hard against falling in love with Sonny because he's also with the police department. But Sonny was very persistent once he realized he was in love with her. Angie is expecting Sonny's first child. Then there's my brother, Teddy. His wife's name is Quinn. And last but not least is my sister Lisa. She's the baby of the family. She just moved out of my parents' home and got an apartment of her own. My mother wasn't thrilled to let her go."

Kelsey thought about how wonderful it would be to have siblings. She didn't have much of a family. All she had now was her mother. Her grandmother had died years ago and she didn't see her father very much. Of course, there was Charlie.

"Teddy and Quinn are real opposites. Teddy's a fly-by-the-seat-of-his-pants type of guy—"

"Like you?" Kelsey interrupted.

Frankie smiled. "So you've figured that out."

"Yes."

"The difference is that when Teddy goes flying he always manages to grab a gold ring."

"I suppose that means he's made a lot of money."

"He's done all right."

"Why didn't you ask him for a loan to buy out your partner?"

"Male ego," Frankie answered lightly. "Do you know anything about male egos?"

Kelsey shook her head, but she had a sense of his predicament. She expected that he was looking to prove himself to his family. "What's Teddy's wife like?"

Frankie tilted his head to the side. "You're a little like Quinn. She's also structured."

"If Quinn is like me and Teddy is like you, what made them right for each other?" After a breath, Kelsey added, "Don't tell me the Italian thunderbolt story again."

Frankie laughed. "Teddy and Quinn did have trouble blending at first. They got divorced three months after they were married. Then they got married again after Quinn gave birth to Teddy's son, TJ. Quinn's expecting their second child now." Frankie drank the last of his beer. "Don't you believe opposites attract?"

"Attraction is one thing. Falling in love is something else. It's hard to know when it isn't just attraction."

"Were you sure you were in love with Eric and not just attracted?"

"Are you sure you're in love with your girlfriend and not just attracted?"

Frankie glanced at his watch. "Do you know that it's almost three in the morning?"

"Really?" The information brought a yawn to Kelsey's lips that she tried to hide with the palm of her hand.

Frankie came around the table and pulled Kelsey to her feet. "Come on, sleepyhead. You're going to bed."

Kelsey wasn't about to fight the idea. "You're going to take the bedroom. We agreed."

"I didn't agree." He tugged her gently.

"Wait a minute." Kelsey pulled back against his hold. "There is a very big bed in there. . . ."

"So?" Frankie asked when she hesitated.

Kelsey finished hemming and hawing with herself. "I suppose we could share it."

"It's okay with me," he said, flipping her a grin. "Why don't you go in and change first? Then you can get under the covers."

"I'm going to sleep in a pair of shorts and a T-shirt," Kelsey responded, trying to sound blasé. "What do you sleep in?"

Frankie knew he was going to do it before he did it. He couldn't help himself. "I sleep in the buff. Just keep your eyes closed."

"What?" Kelsey wasn't absolutely certain he was teasing.

Frankie gave her a wink. "I have shorts with me."

Kelsey's heart was still beating quickly. "Outdoor shorts or boxer shorts?"

"Both. Which do you prefer?"

She shot him an expressive, extended look before she walked off to the bedroom.

When Frankie strolled in, having given her a twenty-minute head start, he saw that Kelsey was under the covers. She'd positioned herself as close as she could get to one side of the bed, giving him a good six-foot clearance.

Through the fringe of her vision, and the light of the lamp on her side, Kelsey watched Frankie open his suitcase. She had to raise her head a little to check out his selection. He took out a pair of khaki shorts and went into the bathroom.

Frankie came back into the bedroom ten minutes later. Careful not to have him spot her, Kelsey took quick note, then immediately shut her eyes. He'd left on the white undershirt he'd been wearing under his dress shirt, and he had the khaki shorts on.

"Are you asleep?" Frankie asked, getting into the bed on his side.

"Yes," Kelsey answered.

"Do you want me to come around and turn out the light?"

"Oh..." Kelsey reached out and clicked off the lamp.

"Sweet dreams," Frankie whispered, his hands locked behind his head.

"You, too," Kelsey whispered back.

It took Kelsey more than half an hour to get her body into a relaxed state. She was very aware of him in the bed with her. "Don't roll," Kelsey said to herself, right before she dozed off.

Even after Kelsey was asleep, Frankie was still trying to force his own body to slow down. He had enjoyed kidding with her and introducing her to the sights of Vegas. He thought about taking her around New York, and hoped that Charlie hadn't already shown her everything there was to see when she'd visited eight months ago. It was funny the way fate worked.... Charlie might have introduced them the first time she'd come to the States, but he hadn't.

Frankie turned his head to look out through the haze of neon, and saw that it was raining. There was a small boom in the distance, and then a flash. A bolt of lightning momentarily brightened the sky.

What a honeymoon this had turned out to be.

Chapter Three

Frankie's watch alarm went off at exactly 9:00 a.m., startling him awake. Quickly he moved to shut the alarm off, when he realized his other arm was pinned beneath Kelsey's back. She was sound asleep. He had to settle for hitting his watch against his chin and, blessedly, the buzzing ceased.

From her even breathing, Frankie could tell that Kelsey had not been bothered by the alarm. They had an 11:00 a.m. flight to catch back to New York, however, and he knew he should wake her. He had no idea how long it took her to get ready.

Kelsey turned in her sleep and snuggled her head in the crook of Frankie's neck. Where their bodies touched near his rib cage, he could tell that she'd gone to bed with her bra on. Frankie smiled. Was that supposed to be protection against a case of roving hands?

Kelsey gave another toss. One of her legs came up and dropped down over both of his. Frankie took a very deep breath and held it for the count of three.

"Kelsey," Frankie whispered into her hair. "Time to rise and shine." That was a Freudian slip if he'd ever heard one.

"Umm," Kelsey murmured.

Frankie raised his head and blew into her ear. He was trying not to startle her.

"Don't," Kelsey complained after a long sigh. She was having a really great dream about an endless stream of quarters pouring out of a slot machine. Frankie was standing there—very close by. He had a chain around his neck with a dice cube hanging from it. Kelsey tried to remember what he'd done to win.... Then she remembered. He'd won for sex appeal.

Frankie nipped at Kelsey's earlobe with his teeth.

Her eyes popped open to the sight of Frankie's face right above hers. She blinked her eyes, then tried for a second look. Her eyes focused. "What are you doing?"

"Trying to behave myself," Frankie said, winking. He used his knee to jiggle the leg she still had thrown over him.

Kelsey shot to a sitting position, taking her misbehaving leg off him. "Did you...ah...?"

"Only in my head," Frankie answered as Kelsey scooted to her side of the bed.

"Did I...?" She suddenly realized she might have been giving him a good touch.

Smiling, Frankie responded, "It doesn't count if you have to ask."

Kelsey turned her face away as it grew red. His girlfriend should just see the two of them now!

"Should we toss a coin to see who gets the bathroom first?" He addressed the back of her head.

"No," Kelsey answered, sliding her feet off the side of the bed. "I'll go first."

"Merciless woman," Frankie groaned comically.

"All right," she reconsidered. "I'll go first. Then you can go, but I get to shower first."

"Better." He laughed.

"What time is it?" Kelsey asked without looking back at him as she moved to the bathroom door. She could still feel the heat in her face.

"A few minutes after nine."

"I'd better not take time to wash my hair," she said, voicing her thoughts out loud.

And he thought about how he'd wanted to see her with her hair all wet and her face shiny clean.

"What would you like for breakfast?" Frankie raised his voice so she could hear him through the closed door. "I'll call down to room service."

"Tea and toast," Kelsey yelled back, turning on the faucet full blast, hoping to drown out the sounds of her morning rituals and gain some sense of privacy.

Out of the corner of his eye Frankie watched Kelsey put her makeup on. He was standing in front of one sink using his electric shaver. She was standing in front of the other. They were sharing the large mirror over the double vanity.

"We agreed not to watch each other," Kelsey reprimanded, catching him. It had been her stipulation, not his, although she snuck in a few peripheral glances herself. This was the first time she'd been with a male when he was shaving. It was a rather interesting process.

"I'm not watching you," Frankie replied innocently, tipping his head to work his shaver over the opposite side of his jaw.

Kelsey rolled her eyes for him in the mirror to let him know she was onto his game. His hair was still wet, and was combed slickly back. He'd dressed in jeans and a black polo shirt that didn't have a slogan on its front and there was a damp towel slung around his neck.

He smiled at her crookedly. "What was that you just put on?"

"It's my sun-blocking cream. If you want to use some you can." She didn't think that with his olive-toned skin he'd really need it. However, her fair complexion didn't take very kindly to the sun.

Frankie picked up the tube as she put it down. He took a sniff. "I'll pass." He put the tube back down. "I don't think I care to be a girly-man."

"Girly-man?" Kelsey grinned while applying a light base of liquid luminescent foundation over her face.

"Don't you get 'Saturday Night Live' in London? It's a TV show." He watched her apply whatever it was she was using and couldn't help thinking that she didn't need to improve on nature.

"It might be on the telly, but I haven't seen it."

"Then we have a date for next Saturday night. Eleven-thirty." Frankie finished shaving and cut the power on his razor.

"I thought you worked most nights late at your—" She'd been about to say pub, then remembered the American term. "Bar."

"I'll arrange to be off next Saturday night." He opened a bottle of after-shave, poured some out in the palm of one hand and rubbed his hands together.

Kelsey watched Frankie slap his palms to his face. She brushed a hint of blush to her cheeks. The aroma of his after-shave filled her nostrils. Citrus, blended with a touch of something just barely sweet. Pleasant, she thought, even though she wasn't breathing all that naturally.

"Do you want me to pour out your tea?" Frankie asked after he'd finished cleaning and packing away his electric shaver.

"Yes." Kelsey regarded his retreating form in the mirror as she used her light coral lipstick. His jeans fit his body extremely well. Just how much of the night had she spent cuddling with him? How much of the night had he been aware of her cuddling up against him?

After their more than fitful night's sleep, Kelsey and Frankie slept almost the entire flight from Las Vegas to New York.

"This is the plan," Frankie said as they each collected their one small suitcase at the baggage-claim area. "We'll swing by the bar first. You can get the key to his apartment from your grandfather. We'll pick up the rest of your things, and then go to my place." He had his car parked at the terminal.

"Did you ever tell me whether you had one bed-room or two?" Kelsey asked, trying to tear a page out of his book of nonchalance.

"One bedroom—" Frankie intentionally paused "—and a convertible couch in the living room that opens into a bed. I'll take the living room, unless you want to share the bed?"

"Will you please remember that you have a girl-friend," Kelsey retorted, flashing him a look of ad-monishment.

"I'm sure you'll remind me if I forget." Frankie winked, deciding to himself that what she needed was a new man in her life. Not that it was going to be him. He had other fish to fry. Besides, he expected that she didn't feel ready for another relationship just yet. She'd probably balk if he tried. "By the way, I've been thinking that the less people that know our marriage is just an arrangement, the better off we'll be." He didn't want anyone to find out the truth. They'd re-ally think he'd flipped out. "Let's keep it between the three of us. You, me and your grandfather. Immigra-tion might very well interview people we come into contact with."

Kelsey nodded, pleased at the way he was concern-ing himself with her goal in all this.

"What do you think?" Frankie asked as they stood in the living room of his apartment. It was a third-floor walk-up in a nicely maintained, rent-controlled, six-story building. He didn't live far from the South Street Seaport and the Fulton Street Fish Market.

"It's very nice," Kelsey answered, very uncomfort-able as she glanced around. The covering on the couch was an uninspired beige weave. The floors were hardwood, covered in the center with an area rug in muted print. There were two armchairs, one a combination of green and beige with a footrest, the other imitation brown leather. A wall unit containing stereo equipment and a TV finished off the room, leaving a considerable amount of open space. The windows, and there were a number of them, were covered only with horizontal blinds, all pulled up halfway. He'd turned the window-unit air conditioner on right after he'd put on the light. It was nearly eight-thirty and getting dark out.

Frankie picked up Kelsey's two large suitcases, which he'd placed on the floor, and led the way to the bedroom.

He hit the light switch and turned another window-unit air conditioner on. Kelsey took in the double bed, requisite nightstands, a moderate-size bureau and a second TV, smaller than the one in the living room, this one on a rolling cart.

Did he really sleep in the buff? The thought came unbidden to her mind.

"I've cleaned the closet out for you." Frankie went to it and opened the door.

"Where are your clothes?"

"I hung up my things in the hall closet. The bureau is all yours, as well."

"I feel like I'm putting you out," Kelsey said inanely. Standing with him in his bedroom was decidedly awkward.

Frankie sent Kelsey a teasing grin, then commented, "Charlie was shocked that we actually went through with it. But his reaction looked right. Everyone else will assume he knew nothing about this."

Kelsey nodded, fidgeting in place. They'd been congratulated by all of Frankie's help at the bar, as well as his soon-to-be ex-partner. Everyone had been shocked at their elopement. His waitresses had thought it was terribly romantic.

Frankie deposited Kelsey's suitcases in front of the closet. "Come on, I'll show you the bathroom and the kitchen."

Kelsey put down the small suitcase that she'd brought with her to Las Vegas, and the other one that she'd packed up at Charlie's apartment with all her photography equipment. Quickly, she followed him out of the bedroom.

"Bathroom." Frankie opened a door right off the living room.

Kelsey peeked in over his shoulder as he put the light on. It was an overly large room for a bathroom. The fixtures were white, and there were black-and-white tiles on the floor and partway up the walls. A dark green plastic shower curtain hung along the tub, and there was a mat in the same color in front of it. She thought about him showering. That would naturally be in the buff. . . .

"Linen closet." Frankie pulled open a small door. He pictured her standing in his tub showering, but he didn't let that picture get too detailed.

Kelsey nodded, not taking much of a look.

"The kitchen is small," Frankie pointed out unnecessarily when they arrived in the room. "I usually eat at the bar, or I pick up takeout when I eat at home. Did you have enough to eat before?"

Charlie had insisted that they sit down while they were at the bar and tell them about their short excursion to Las Vegas. He'd served them the special he'd cooked for the day. Roasted quarters of chicken with mashed potatoes and broccoli.

"I'm full." She'd eaten as much as she needed to eat not to fade away. She'd seen Frankie do justice to his meal. Nothing seemed to get in the way of his appetite.

"I haven't gotten around to stocking up on staples." Frankie stuck his hands into the back pockets of his jeans. "We can go grocery shopping tomorrow."

"When are you going back to work?" Kelsey observed the stretch of his shirt across his shoulder blades now that he'd taken up a new stance.

"Thursday. I'm taking the next couple of days off."

Kelsey drew her gaze up to his face. "Because of me?"

"I'm due a short break." He wanted to make sure she was acclimatized.

Kelsey responded with a nod. This moving into his apartment was turning out to be even more difficult than she'd anticipated. Had he told his girlfriend that this marriage of theirs was just a scheme? She wasn't clear on that point. He had said they should keep the real reason for this marriage between them and Charlie. But surely he must have told his girlfriend. Would she be coming around to see him?

"Well . . ." Frankie took his hands out of his pockets and leaned back against one of the white-painted cabinets. "Have you ever lived with anyone else?"

"Other than my parents?" Kelsey knew that wasn't what he meant.

"Other than your parents?"

"No. Have you?"

Frankie answered with a negative quirk of his head. It was a question he probably shouldn't have asked.

"I'm not going to consider this as living together... because we're not really living together." Kelsey recalled the compromising position she'd been in with him when she'd woken up in the morning, and felt a flash of heat.

"If you're not going to count it, I won't count it, either," Frankie teased. "Are you tired?"

"No. Are you tired?"

"No." He was wired, not tired. "I'm going to have to tell my parents that their second and only other son has bitten the bullet."

It took Kelsey a second to convert his slang to English. "Do you mean tonight?"

"I can go over myself. I'll say you're wiped out, but you will have to meet them sometime soon, and there is the rest of the clan."

Kelsey chewed her bottom lip. "Where do your parents live?"

"Brooklyn... a half hour from here."

Their eyes connected. He tried some sweet-talking with his. Hers narrowed, considered, then leveled.

"I'll go with you," Kelsey decided. It didn't make sense to put off the inevitable. The pulse in her neck was beating so hard she wouldn't have been surprised if he could see it. It was that close to the surface of her throat.

Frankie let his mouth hint at a grin. "I was hoping I looked pathetic enough."

"You did." Kelsey rolled her eyes for him.

Frankie had to park on the street in front of his parents' brick home in Bensonhurst. There was an extra car in the driveway. He recognized it as his Uncle Joey's car, which of course meant that his Aunt Nettie was also inside. He should have called first.

Kelsey looked over at Frankie. The sun was entirely down, but there were streetlights and she could see him clearly enough. He'd turned the engine off, but he was just sitting behind the wheel.

"Are you nervous?" Kelsey asked. She'd gone beyond nervous ten minutes ago.

Frankie shook his head, though it belied his true feelings. "An aunt and uncle of mine are over. We're a very large family. Did I mention that?"

"You told me about your siblings and your brothers-in-law and your sister-in-law. I expect I should jot down their names with a bit of description to keep them straight in my head for immigration."

"Get a big notebook." Frankie took a breath and then got out of the car.

Kelsey had just gotten one foot out from her side of the car as Frankie came around to meet her. She hadn't been waiting for him to assist her. It was trepidation that had her moving slowly.

He took her hand, aiding her the rest of the way out. Kelsey didn't object. Nor did she object when he continued to hold her hand as they walked along the slate path to the front steps. There was a light on overhead, and Kelsey glanced at Frankie just as he looked over at her. The gazes of the two conspirators fastened together.

Kelsey made a proposal. "How about if I go back to the car and wait until you've told them, then you can come and get me?"

He grinned, "Actually, I think it would be most effective if I carried you in over the threshold. That would make a statement without my having to say too much."

She jammed an elbow into his side.

Connie Falco opened the door to Frankie's knock. "I didn't expect to see you tonight." She smiled at her son, and then looked interestedly at Kelsey. Kelsey saw a short woman with narrow shoulders and generous hips. Her gray hair was cut becomingly close to her face. She was wearing a cotton housedress in a summer print. She looked invitingly warm.

"Do we get to come in?" Frankie asked jokingly.

"Frankie's here," Connie called out, which was entirely needless since the other three people in the house could see both Frankie and Kelsey as they came in. The foyer opened right into the living room where the others were sitting.

"Everyone," Frankie said in greeting, "this is Kelsey." He had to tug on her hand to get her to move forward.

Along with Connie, the other three members of the family were now on their feet.

"Kelsey," Frankie said, "this is my father, Anthony Falco."

A tall, thin man with a full head of gray hair shook Kelsey's hand.

Kelsey knew her palm was damp.

"This is my Aunt Nettie, one of my mother's sisters," Frankie continued.

"Hello," Aunt Nettie said.

"Hello," Kelsey returned, seeing the family resemblance between the two women.

"And this is my Uncle Joey."

Short, bald and rotund, Uncle Joey gave Kelsey's hand a vigorous pump.

"And, of course, my mother." Frankie finished the introductions.

"We'll go in the kitchen," Connie Falco said, ever the hostess. "I'll make more coffee. I baked cheesecake today."

"Not right now, Ma," Frankie said.

Connie, Anthony, Nettie and Joey went back to their seats.

Frankie continued to stand. Kelsey continued to stand. His arm came around her. Frankie took a breath. Kelsey held hers.

"Kelsey and I got married yesterday," Frankie announced.

"Anthony..." Connie clapped a hand to her chest. "Did he say that he got married yesterday?"

Frankie's father was speechless.

Nettie answered, "Connie, he got married yesterday."

"Frankie, Frankie, Frankie," came Uncle Joey's input.

Four pairs of wide eyes fixed on Kelsey.

Kelsey couldn't decide where to look, so she dropped her gaze to her feet. She was wearing sandals.

"Kelsey is from London. She's Charlie Peterson's granddaughter," Frankie said, trying to fill in the silence.

"You went to London?" Connie questioned in confusion. "When did you go to London? I spoke to you two days ago."

"I didn't go to London, Ma," Frankie grinned. "I met Kelsey eight months ago when she came to see her grandfather—"

Anthony Falco finally found his voice. "That's Charlie Peterson. We've met him a few times. Nice man."

"Yes, Dad." Frankie nodded. "Anyway, we went out when she was here eight months ago. Ten nights in a row. She hooked me right then and there, but she wouldn't believe me. Right, sweetheart?" Not getting any response, Frankie repeated, "Sweetheart?"

"Let go of her and let her sit down," Connie scolded her son. "You're making her nervous." Connie patted the cushion on the plastic-covered pale blue couch between where she and Anthony sat. "Come here, sweetheart."

Frankie dropped his arm from around Kelsey. "Sure, leave me to take the inquisition alone."

Connie patted the couch again. "Don't pay any attention to him. He's a scooch."

Frankie laughed. "She's not Italian, Ma."

"A tease," Connie Falco paraphrased as Kelsey sat in the seat she'd been directed to.

Kelsey nodded to her new mother-in-law. "Yes, he is."

"He's not fooling around now, is he?" Connie asked Kelsey.

"No." Kelsey shook her head.

"Do you like him?" the older woman asked, adding without a break, "You have to like each other as much as you love each other. My mother said that to me the night before I married Frankie's father."

Kelsey nodded her head. It was a wonderful thought—it had nothing to do with her and Frankie, but it was a wonderful thought.

Connie threw her arms around Kelsey and hugged. Not expecting such elation, Kelsey was totally startled. "Anthony, we have another daughter!" Connie exclaimed.

Smiling, Frankie asked, "Don't I get to say anything more?"

With an arm around Kelsey, Connie replied, "What do you have to tell me—that you didn't invite us to the wedding?"

"We went to Vegas, Ma. Just the two of us."

"You couldn't wait two minutes for us to pack a bag?"

"Just like Teddy," Anthony remarked. "They see the woman they want and they don't know from anything else. They can't wait two minutes."

"I'll call Vinnie. He goes to sleep early when his hall is closed. Then we'll really get to know each other." Connie let go of a harried Kelsey as she got up from the couch.

"I'm going back to work on Thursday," Frankie informed his mother as he took the place she had vacated on the couch.

"My freezer is stocked," Nettie said to her sister Connie.

"Mine, too," Connie responded, walking to her kitchen with Nettie catching up. "Fran will have to start cooking. She never prepares ahead."

Kelsey glanced at Frankie, trying to decipher the exchange that had just gone on between the two older women. There wasn't any clue on his face. What there was on his face was the most adoring looking she'd ever received from any male. Kelsey stared back at him mutely, startled afresh. She hadn't given any thought to how he planned to behave toward her around his family.

Smiling, Anthony Falco motioned to his brother-in-law, "Look at the two of them. Can't take their eyes off each other. Remember when . . ."

"Ah, *amore*," Uncle Joey said.

Without warning, Frankie's hand came from behind to circle Kelsey's waist, nestling her closely to him—thigh to thigh. "*Amore* and a lot of chemistry," Frankie quipped.

Oh, my God! Kelsey thought, blushing at the unmistakably seductive look Frankie was giving her now. What had she gotten herself into?

Chapter Four

"I do need my chocolate chip cookies to get me through the week," Frankie said to Kelsey as they stood in the supermarket aisle the next morning. He dumped two bags of the cookies in question into their cart. "Do you like sweets?"

"No, but I do like pretzels." Kelsey grabbed a bag and added it to the cart. "If you see me eating too many, take them away from me. Okay?"

"You don't have to worry about eating too many."

"Are you saying that you think I'm too skinny?" After asking the question, Kelsey wondered if she might have asked it intentionally, hoping he would compliment her again. Her breasts were small, barely a B cup, but she'd been told, regardless of that, that she had a good figure.

Frankie gave Kelsey a rapscallion grin. "That's not what I'm saying."

"What are you saying?" Now she really wanted to know what he thought.

"Does it matter to you what I think?" He deliberately looked her over. She was wearing jeans and a polo, just like he was.

"Not in the least." With feigned indifference Kelsey began pushing the cart farther down the aisle.

"What there is of you works for me," Frankie whispered behind her back. "But you are a little skinny."

"Would you please keep your mind on this shopping," Kelsey countered hypocritically, having reminded herself that he had a girlfriend...not that she was looking to get involved with him. The last thing she wanted in her life right now was any man. Especially a man who also happened to be her husband.

"I didn't get to see this section of New York when I was here last time," Kelsey said, excitedly snapping pictures. They were in the South Street Seaport, having finished their shopping and put their groceries away back at the apartment.

"Look over there," Frankie directed as they stood outdoors on the second level of the mall area. "That's the Statue of Liberty. It's a little far but you can make it out."

"I was there with Charlie," Kelsey said, getting a telephoto lens from the knapsack she was carrying. "This could be an interesting shot." She snapped one, and then as Frankie watched she climbed up on one of the benches close to the rail over the East River.

Frankie quickly grabbed hold of Kelsey's hips as she tilted forward. "I thought you said you weren't daring." She'd just about given him a heart attack.

Kelsey took her camera from her eye to look down at him. "I said I wasn't daring in my thinking. Angling to get a shot has nothing to do with being daring. I'm pretty agile, which is a benefit to being skinny."

Frankie laughed. "I'll consider myself told off, but could you please not angle as much?"

Kelsey came down from the bench with the assistance of Frankie's hands still on her hips. "You can let go of me now," she informed him.

Frankie dropped his hands to his sides. "How about some lunch?"

"Okay, but dutch." She opened her knapsack to put her camera away.

"You are a cheap date." Frankie grinned.

"I'm not a date." Before she thought to stop herself, she added, "I'm your wife...in name only." How was she supposed to behave with a man who was her husband, but wasn't really her husband, and was someone else's boyfriend?

Frankie retorted, "I've got to tell you, you are cramping my style and my principles. My father brought his sons up to pay for any woman we were out with."

In Kelsey's opinion he had more style than he needed but she didn't mention that.

"How about the place right over there for lunch?" Frankie asked.

"Okay," she agreed.

The place Frankie had suggested was a Western bar. Even at midday it was hopping with couples doing the two-step to a live band. Waiters were rushing around carrying trays of southern fried chicken.

They found their table—one just vacated close to where the band was playing. Kelsey gazed raptly at the dancers while her head caught the rhythm of the music.

"Do you like to dance?" Frankie asked, watching her bop her head.

"Yes, but I don't know how to dance to this. Do you?"

"No, but I'm game to give it a try if you are."

"I don't think so." Kelsey widened her eyes at him.

Frankie reached out and got his fingers under her hair. He gave her one earring a gentle tug.

"I thought you wanted to start being more daring," he challenged her.

Kelsey lightly slapped his hand away from her ear. "Daring is one thing, deliberately trying to make a fool of myself is something else."

"I'd be leaving myself open, as well," Frankie noted.

"That's true." Kelsey deliberated. "Wait a minute... How do I know that you don't really know how to dance to this?"

Frankie grinned. "There's only one way for you to find out. Tell you what, I'll order us a drink while you think about it. What would you like to have?" He put up his hand to catch the eye of whoever was in charge of their table.

"Ice tea," Kelsey answered immediately.

"You really are structured," Frankie teased. Since his hand wasn't catching them any service, he said, "I'll go get it from the bar."

Kelsey looked around when Frankie took off. It was a weekday and the place was full. Didn't anyone go to work in New York?

Frankie came back a few minutes later with Kelsey's ice tea, a beer for himself and two menus. Kelsey asked him the question she'd just asked herself.

"It's lunchtime. The people you see here no doubt all work either here at the mall or close by." He handed her one of the menus he'd picked up from the bar. "Have you decided if you want to get out on the dance floor with me?" He didn't know the two-step, but he did like to dance.

"I'm still thinking about it." Kelsey opened her menu. Then she closed it. "All right, I'll try it with you. But if it turns out that I'm the only one who makes a fool of themselves, I'm not going to speak to you for the rest of the day."

"Promises, promises," Frankie kidded as he got to his feet and Kelsey got to hers.

She gave him a silly smirk in return. "Let's stay to the outside edge."

"Okay." Frankie took her hand and led her forward.

They waited at the sideline for the start of a tune, watching the other couples, individually trying to catch on to the steps. When the song ended and a new one began, Frankie held her in a dance position.

"It looks to me like it's a combination of square dancing and close dancing," Frankie said as he took a step forward and took a step back.

"What is square dancing?" Kelsey asked.

"Never mind, I don't know how to square dance, either," was Frankie's instant reply. He didn't care for square dancing, but he had tried it once or twice.

Kelsey's body and Frankie's body caught the movement faster than their feet. They stepped on each other's toes a few times. Their legs tangled once and they had to hold on to each other to keep from toppling over. But by their third song they had it down pat. Frankie twirled Kelsey out and reeled her back in. They were smiling at each other as they got winded.

"Do you want to sit down and eat now?" Frankie asked.

"Yes," Kelsey answered, quite ready.

They took their seats again. The place had emptied out somewhat. They'd only looked at their menus briefly when a waiter approached.

"Are you ready to order?" He was young with dirty blond hair and blue eyes.

"Do you know what you want?" Frankie asked, watching Kelsey glance up at their waiter. He wondered what type of guy she went for.... He wondered what Eric looked like....

"That chicken everyone seems to be eating smells wonderful," Kelsey answered.

"Make it two," Frankie said.

"Fries or mashed potatoes?" their waiter asked.

"Mashed potatoes," Kelsey responded.

"Fries," Frankie replied.

The food arrived incredibly fast and, for the first time since he'd met her, Frankie watched Kelsey eat with an appetite. The portions were huge. Even he couldn't finish all his.

Her stomach filled to capacity, Kelsey looked down at all that was still left on her plate. "It was so good I hate to leave any of it."

Frankie solved that problem by having what they'd both left over packed up so they could take it back to the apartment. Then they divided the check at Kelsey's insistence.

Frankie complained. "If anyone I know sees me taking money from you like this, they're going to think I've become a gigolo. How about we take turns? You treat me. I treat you."

"I don't think we should plan on going out together that often." She'd made up some ground rules in her mind for this arrangement between them. That was one of them.

Her remark rankled him. "Whatever." Frankie shrugged impassively. "I'll run back home and put the chicken away. You can keep on taking pictures. I'll meet you back outside by the benches."

Kelsey was aware that he'd suddenly turned cool toward her. She would have expected him to understand that socializing the way they had been wasn't the best of ideas. How exactly would he have explained it to his girlfriend. How exactly would she have explained it to her racing pulse?

Kelsey cleaned off her side of the table in Frankie's kitchen after having eaten what had been left of her chicken for dinner. Frankie did the same on his end. Kelsey dumped her scraps into the garbage can under the sink, then washed her plate and silverware. Frankie did the same. There hadn't been much conversation between them since lunch. She'd taken two rolls of film at the South Street Seaport. A few times she'd wanted to ask if he would mind if she took a shot or two of him, wanting a subject she could pose for some of her frames. But she'd quashed the thought every time it had come into her mind.

"Is there anything you'd like to do this evening?" Frankie asked, but only because he felt he should. He was still ticked off with her.

"You don't have to concern yourself with entertaining me." She knew her words may have sounded harsh but all she was trying to tell him was that she didn't want to interfere in his life.

Frankie walked out of the kitchen, and Kelsey heard him turn on the TV. With nothing in the kitchen for her to do, she moved into the living room. She saw that he was seated on the couch, so she sat in one of the armchairs. They watched a news broadcast from seven-thirty to eight. A cops-and-robbers show came on next on the same channel and they watched that.

"Well..." Kelsey said as the network went into a commercial break. "I'm going to turn in now." When he looked over at her, Kelsey put a hand to her mouth and faked a yawn.

"Good night," Frankie responded impersonally. The yawn she'd just favored him with had been a put-on if he'd ever seen one.

"I suppose we should have a bathroom schedule," Kelsey said, getting to her feet. "I mean for showering and all."

"I can shower in the morning or at night. It makes no difference to me."

She was miserable with his present attitude. "I'll shower in the morning."

"Fine." Frankie raised a shoulder indifferently.

Kelsey didn't bother to say good-night. He seemed to be already engrossed in the next show on the telly.

He heard her put the television on in the bedroom after she'd closed the door. She had it on low, but he could make out the hum. He got up from the couch in a very irritated mood, yanked the cushions off and opened the convertible up. He went to the hall closet and got the pillows and the blanket he'd placed there. He went into the bathroom and got linens for himself out of the small closet, then quickly made his bed up.

The bedroom TV was still on three-quarters of an hour later, after he'd finished taking a long shower. Wearing a pair of shorts, he got into his bed and turned the living room TV back on. He watched a ball game without enjoying it, though his team won.

Finally, around midnight, he heard her turn off the TV in the bedroom—a half hour after he'd turned the living room TV off.

What had she suddenly found objectionable about his company? And why did it bother him so much?

Chapter Five

"How many people do you think will be in there?" Kelsey asked anxiously, sitting alongside Frankie in his car.

Frankie maneuvered a sharp left-hand turn before answering, "Given there was less than a day's notice, I'd say maybe thirty to forty. My mother and father both come from large families and most of them live in the boroughs or Long Island. There would be more if it wasn't for summer vacations. A number of them will be away."

"I feel awful having your parents spend money making a party for us. You should have talked them out of it."

"There isn't a lot of money involved. My Uncle Vinnie often opens his catering hall for the family to use for get-togethers on a weeknight. My mother and aunts cleaned out their freezers and brought the food.

I sent over wine and champagne from the bar, and the band is auditioning. My family gets together at the drop of a hat. My mother is in her glory at being in charge. Does that make it all right now?"

"That's a bit of a relief," she answered without feeling relieved. It had been hard enough meeting his mother and father and just one set of aunts and uncles. It wasn't that she hadn't liked them. She'd really liked them, and that added to her dismay. Her conscience was giving her a problem. Now there were thirty or forty more people to fool.

Frankie took his attention off the street and his driving to send Kelsey a glance. She was wearing the dress they'd gotten married in. "By the way, you look very nice."

"Thank you," Kelsey replied politely, avoiding eye contact. "You look very nice yourself." He was also wearing his wedding attire—navy blazer, blue slacks, blue shirt, though his tie was now a splashy pattern of orange, yellow and lime.

"Thank you." He trotted his manners out for her in the same formal way she'd trotted hers out for him. "I thought it went well at the immigration office this morning."

"Yes," Kelsey answered. He'd already said that to her, and she'd already responded that the application had been easy enough. "I wonder how long it will take for them to put an agent on the case?"

"It looked like they were pretty busy down there."

Two blocks up and one block after a right, Frankie turned the radio on, tuning in a soft rock station to break the silence.

An Elvis Presley song came on. Kelsey instantly thought of the fun they'd had going around Las Vegas on their wedding night. The South Street Seaport had been fun yesterday, too—until after lunch. He was still being cool toward her.

Frankie considered changing the station, but decided against it. He cast her another glance. "What would you do if Eric got in touch with you and said he'd started divorce proceedings?"

His question, coming out of the blue as it did, startled Kelsey. "Do you mean right now?" She wasn't sure what he was getting at.

"Let's say at the end of our arrangement. After you have your green card. Would you pick up with him again?"

Kelsey fiddled with the clutch bag in her lap. "I don't know. I guess I'd have to think about it." She suddenly realized she hadn't thought about Eric at all these past couple of days. That surprised her.

Frankie gritted his teeth. "I can't believe you'd even think about it." The idea of her carrying a torch annoyed him no end, which was confusing since he wasn't personally looking to make a play for her.

"Is this any of your business?" Kelsey's emotions were simmering.

"I guess not." Frankie put his elbow on the frame of the opened window and, agitated, tapped the roof of his hatchback.

"Speaking of business," Kelsey retorted, "I would prefer that you stop touching me the way you did when we were at your parents'."

Striking an amicable chord with her was like trying to squeeze toothpaste out of an empty tube. He'd stroked her arm a few times for show. He'd given her a light kiss on her cheek once...maybe twice. He'd put his arm around her shoulders on the way out.

"I'll drop it from the act," Frankie drawled. "Though it's going to be pretty hard to pretend we're in love without some of the classic moves. I suppose you'd also like me to stop looking at you like I can't wait to get you alone."

Kelsey was embarrassed that he was bringing that out in the open. Her cheeks pinkened just thinking about the looks in question. He'd treated her to them a number of times when they were at his parents' house.

"I thought your blushing the way you are now was just the right touch," Frankie continued offhandedly. "If you want me to stop it, now is the time to say so."

"First of all, I am not blushing. It's warm out. And I don't even know what looks you're talking about, but if you want to stop doing them it's all right with me."

"No touching and no looking." Frankie killed the motor, having pulled in to a parking space in the lot of his Uncle Vinnie's catering hall. "How do you suggest that we try and pull this off?" He shifted in his seat, putting his back to the door to face her.

"I have no idea."

"If you come up with something, just let me know." Frankie put a hand behind him and opened his car door.

Kelsey knew he was exasperated with her. She was exasperated with him. She opened her own door and stepped out.

They met at the front of the car. As Kelsey started to walk, Frankie put his hand on her upper arm and halted her. He took his hand off her as soon as he'd prompted her to turn toward him. He'd planned on being charming and friendly with her tonight. After all, he was dragging her into a room full of his family.

"What?" Kelsey asked, not offering him even a glance.

Frankie stuffed his hands into the pockets of his jacket. "Look, I'm sorry. What just happened between us was all my fault. I don't know what got into me, but my timing really stinks. Can we start again?"

Kelsey stared down at the ground, rolling a pebble with the toe of her shoe. Slowly she brought her eyes up to Frankie's face. "Well...ah..."

"What?" Frankie noticed that the haze off Sheepshead Bay made her sand-colored hair shimmer.

She chewed the side of her mouth before she asked, "Could we hold hands going in?"

Frankie put his hand out to her. "I'd like you to know that I think you're being pretty terrific about all of this. I'm sorry about this party. There really wasn't anything I could do about it."

Kelsey's fingers accepted the weave of his. To be fair, this couldn't be that much easier for him than it was for her. "I do realize that we have to act like newlyweds if we're going to both get what we want out of this."

"So this is what marriage is all about," Frankie kidded. "Compromise."

Kelsey's mouth lifted at the corners, giving him the response his teasing her had just earned.

Fingers laced, they entered the building and were greeted at the door by Vinnie Mateo.

"Ah, the bride." Uncle Vinnie gave Kelsey a once-over.

Kelsey's heart bounced around, though she'd told herself as she'd dressed for the night that, in the long run, it wasn't going to matter whether any of his family really liked her.

Frankie held Kelsey's hand tighter.

"You did good," Uncle Vinnie pronounced.

"I know." Frankie bestowed an admiring smile on Kelsey.

Kelsey smiled back on cue, already disjointed within the first second of all this.

"Go on in." Uncle Vinnie shooed them along. "Just about everyone's here."

Frankie propelled Kelsey across the black-and-white-marble lobby. It was lavishly decorated with floral sconces, couches, an assortment of statuettes, wishing wells and waterfalls. Kelsey could just barely take it all in.

A five-piece band was playing in the room they entered. Between the conversations all around and the music, the noise level was high. There was a buffet set up on one side and there were more flowers all around.

"All these flowers," Kelsey whispered in consternation.

"They're not real." Frankie addressed her concern.

Kelsey took a quick breath. She'd hardly exhaled when they were surrounded by three couples.

Frankie sorted the group out. "Kelsey, this is my brother, Teddy. My sister-in-law, Quinn. My sister

Angie. My brother-in-law Sonny. My sister Nancy. My brother-in-law Shep.''

Kelsey acknowledged each introduction with her best-mannered smile. She knew she wouldn't have any trouble remembering that Teddy was Frankie's brother. The two men looked very much alike though Teddy was a bit broader and slightly taller.

Teddy swept Kelsey practically off her feet with a generous hug. "Welcome to the family.''

"Hi." Quinn smiled warmly when Teddy let Kelsey go.

"Hi," Kelsey replied, just catching her breath. She remembered Frankie saying that she reminded him of Teddy's wife, Quinn. Kelsey wished it would have been for appearance' sake. Quinn was beautiful—blond and classy. If Frankie hadn't told her Quinn was pregnant, Kelsey wouldn't have been able to tell.

"We were all beginning to think that Frankie would never settle down," Angie said vivaciously. She was radiant and attractive, with wavy reddish-brown hair and vibrant eyes. She was showing her pregnancy, but still didn't look very far along.

"I knew when he did fall, he'd fall hard," Sonny said with a grin. He had his arm adoringly around his wife's waist.

"Just look at her." Frankie raised an eyebrow in Kelsey's direction. "What chance did I have?"

Kelsey felt herself blush. She'd agreed that they should act like newlyweds, but did he have to lay it on with such aplomb?

"I know how intimidating this all must be," Nancy said. "We've made up to keep an eye on you and res- cue you when it looks like you need rescuing." With her short dark hair and sophisticated flair, Nancy was a perfect complement to her husband's refinement.

"Thank you," Kelsey said, wishing that she wasn't misleading them.

"Listen, if my brother gives you any trouble let me know," Teddy razzed. "I'll straighten him out for you."

"It looks like Frankie is already jumping through hoops," Sonny said.

"You should know." Frankie ribbed his brother and brother-in-law right back. "Angie and Quinn have the two of you dancing in circles."

Angie laughed and beckoned Kelsey with a nod of her head. "Shall we leave them to do their beleaguered-guy thing while we go off and get to know each other?"

"You can have her a little later on," Frankie answered for Kelsey. "We've got to make the rounds. By the way, where's Lisa?"

"She's out on the dance floor with Johnny," Teddy responded, not sounding pleased as he mentioned the name of his youngest sister's date.

Frankie exchanged a look with his brother that verified that he was also displeased. "We'll catch up with you all later," Frankie said and whisked Kelsey away.

"What's wrong with Johnny?" Kelsey inquired, though she was thinking that she probably shouldn't be asking for insider information.

"Johnny and Lisa are always breaking up and getting back together again. None of us feel he's right for her. We'd all like to see Lisa get him out of her system."

"Oh." Kelsey nodded, seeing Frankie in a new role—protective brother. She expected that he'd be a good brother.

They had begun to walk across the room when Connie and Anthony Falco intercepted them.

"Here she is," Frankie's father said excitedly. Taking Kelsey from Frankie, Anthony Falco placed a kiss on each of her cheeks. Kelsey couldn't get over how marvelously warmhearted Frankie's family was.

Connie Falco beamed as she looked on. "We're going to have more beautiful grandchildren from these two."

Kelsey felt her face flush. The idea of her and Frankie accomplishing that particular feat made the muscles in Kelsey's lower abdomen tighten. She did hope that what she was experiencing was merely caused by embarrassment and not anticipation.

"Don't push, Ma." Frankie grinned. "We're not thinking about having a family yet. We just got married." The thought of making love to his bride wasn't something Frankie wanted on his mind. This was the damnedest thing he'd ever been through—all the more absurd because he had a legal right to the thought.

"I'm not pushing," Connie disclaimed. "Anthony, am I pushing?"

"You're not pushing." Anthony backed his wife up.

"What do you think of my granddaughter?" Charlie Peterson asked proudly, coming into the conversation right behind Kelsey.

Kelsey craned her neck to look at her grandfather's evenly featured, jovial face. He could have passed for ten years younger than his early sixties. Had he ever regretted divorcing her grandmother, Kelsey pondered, not for the first time. He'd never married again. Had he been too busy working to have a personal life? She still hadn't decided how much of a relationship she was comfortable having with him. Her mother had insisted that was entirely up to her.

"All we had to do was see them together to know that they're perfect for each other," Connie said, smiling.

Frankie rescued the moment. "I see Lisa at the buffet table. Excuse us, I want Kelsey to meet Lisa."

"Go. Eat something," Connie agreed. "The lasagna, meatballs and calamari salad all the way on the right—" Connie pointed "—is mine. Keep away from your Aunt Fran's meatballs. She's standing at the table dishing them out. I gave one a taste. She used too much oregano, and too much garlic."

Deftly Frankie swung Kelsey away with a tug on her hand. "Are you hungry?"

"I don't know." Her stomach was doing some kind of jig.

They were waylaid every few steps on their way to the buffet table. Frankie introduced Kelsey to cousins, aunts and uncles. Kelsey could not keep up with the names or faces. She was mesmerized by a sensation of the room twirling crazily around her.

As soon as they did get to the buffet table, Frankie reached for two glasses of champagne. He handed one to her, and Kelsey drank hers quickly. Frankie took his time.

"Do you like champagne?" he asked.

"No." Kelsey wiggled her nose against the bubbles she'd just inhaled.

Frankie grinned into her eyes. "Do you like wine?"

"Yes." Kelsey smiled back without thinking about it.

Frankie took Kelsey's empty glass and put it down with his half-full one. He picked up two glasses of wine. "You should probably eat something first before you drink any more."

Kelsey took one of the glasses from him. "I'll just have a sip, then I will."

"There's Lisa," Frankie said, and waved her over.

Kelsey had taken three sips of her wine in the time it took Lisa to reach them. Kelsey was beginning to disconnect from most of her tension.

"Where's Johnny?" Frankie asked, keeping his opinion of his sister's boyfriend from showing.

Lisa made a face. "We had a fight. He left. I don't want to talk about it."

"Kelsey, this is Lisa." Frankie put a solacing arm around his sister's slim shoulders.

"Hi," Kelsey responded, admiring Frankie's concern. Lisa looked more like Frankie and Teddy than she did either of her sisters.

Lisa's smile was quick and winsome. "This is going to be great. Did you meet my sisters? I think of Quinn as a sister, not a sister-in-law. Now there's going to be five of us. We can go shopping together."

Kelsey barely managed a nod.

"Oh." Lisa sighed. "Johnny just came back in." Extricating herself from Frankie's hand, Lisa took off.

Frankie whistled an elongated breath through his teeth before he focused back on Kelsey. "What would you like to eat? Have you ever had lasagna?"

"No, but I'd like to try it."

Frankie found his mother's lasagna and fixed a plate for himself and Kelsey.

Kelsey was halfway through relishing the portion Frankie had cut for her when someone in the band announced it was time for the tarantella.

"We have to dance to this. It's tradition," Frankie said, taking Kelsey's plate away from her.

"I don't know how," she objected strenuously while Frankie tugged her to the dance floor.

"With the way you pick up dance steps, you'll catch right on." He gave her a confident smile.

Kelsey found herself in a circle with Frankie at her right and Teddy at her left. They each took her hand. Before Kelsey had the chance to even ask Frankie what the steps were, she was moving her feet. Knowing the steps didn't seem to matter. She just kept going around and around feeling the fast pace of the music permeate her.

Suddenly Kelsey was whirling around in Frankie's arms, and when he loosened his hold on her they were in the middle of the dance floor surrounded by everyone else. The music became faster and more upbeat. Frankie raised his arms over his head, snapping his fingers, his body still in motion. Guided by his example, Kelsey spun around, snapping her fingers over her head, stamping her feet when he stamped his, swaying her hips the way his hips swayed. Frankie watched hypnotically as Kelsey rotated in front of him, her hips swinging, her hair flying. Her dress twirled out and his eyes caught on her legs, her knees, a glimpse of thighs.

He snared her waist with his arm to spin her. Kelsey was giddy and smiling and Frankie was smiling with her.

The music built to a crescendo and ended with a wild, final blast. Kelsey practically collapsed against Frankie. He held her tightly, supporting her and himself.

"Did...I...do...it...right?" Kelsey asked, taking in gasps of air just over his shoulder.

"Absolutely right," Frankie answered thickly, still seeing the image of her dancing in his mind. She'd been absolutely sensual.

Their eyes made contact. Neither Kelsey nor Frankie were aware that they were all alone. The dance floor had cleared. The band had stopped playing, but there was new noise starting up around them. Lots of noise. The resounding sound of silverware striking wineglasses filled the air.

Kelsey saw Frankie's lips move as he said something to her, but this time she couldn't hear him with the tinkling jangle going on.

"They want me to kiss you," Frankie repeated, trying to think cool thoughts as he put the words to Kelsey's ear. He'd expected to kiss her sometime during the night. It wouldn't have been a wedding reception—even one after the fact—without at least one ceremonial kiss. Only, right now wasn't the best time for him.

Kelsey heard what Frankie said. Frankie heard Kelsey's deep swallow.

Startled, Kelsey looked around to find everyone in the room waiting with their eyes on them. They were still clanking away on their glasses.

"I'll make it quick," Frankie promised at Kelsey's ear. "They're not going to stop until they get what they want."

Before Kelsey had the chance to consider another assault to her senses, Frankie, in exaggerated style, had tilted her backward. Kelsey grabbed the lapels of Frankie's jacket, feeling as if she was about to land on the floor. There was applause at that because it seemed to the crowd that she was encouraging him instead of only trying to hold on. When Frankie's mouth finally dropped down to hers there were hoots and whistles and glasses tapped all the more demandingly.

He'd said he was going to be brief. He'd intended to be brief, but he got hooked once he got there—especially with her lips parting for him. He was a normal, red-blooded American male. A hot and bothered American male.

The champagne, the wine and the way they'd danced together had already gone to Kelsey's head. Was everyone still watching, Kelsey asked herself incoherently, while Frankie gave her a kiss that turned her spine to jelly. He had an awesome talent for this....

Frankie straightened Kelsey back on her two feet as he ended the lip lock, but not before exploring the interior of her accommodating mouth with his tongue—something he knew he shouldn't have done. His logic had stalled out on him, returning only after the fact.

There was still some applause going on around them.

"Looks like they enjoyed it." Frankie smiled.

Kelsey stared at him. She was having a hard time coming up with a suitable comment, but her eyes were talking.

It was her gaze that Frankie zeroed in on. "I know what you're thinking."

"You don't know what I'm thinking," Kelsey replied angrily. She was thinking that he had some nerve kissing her the way he'd kissed her when he had a girlfriend.

"Yes, I do." He didn't need any psychic powers. Her copper eyes were shooting hatchets his way.

"You are a cad!" Kelsey exclaimed.

"Don't you think you're making a little bit much out of a kiss?" Frankie countered, trying to make light of it. He knew the reason she'd given him the epithet, just as he knew why he wasn't going to tell her he was unattached. He wasn't about to buy himself the aggravation of having her think he was eligible and on the make.

Struggling not to let her anger show to the party goers, Kelsey started to head away. Frankie stuck close to her side. He didn't figure she wanted him to hold her hand at the moment.

Chapter Six

After taking her morning shower, Kelsey came out of the bathroom dressed for the day in jeans and an Indian print blouse. She walked the outer fringe of the living room to the bedroom to hang up her fluffy chenille robe and fold away her nightgown. Leaving the bedroom, she could hear that Frankie was in the kitchen.

"Good morning," Frankie said leisurely when Kelsey appeared.

"Good morning," she returned without meeting his gaze. He was having his coffee with a slice of their wedding cake from the portion they'd brought home from the party the night before.

For Kelsey, seeing the wedding cake was like waving a red flag in front of a bull. During the reception she'd had to feed him some and he'd fed her some. Then he'd kissed her again. It had been a shorter kiss, but it had made as much of an impact on her as his first kiss. To top it off, she'd had to slow dance with him three times. Not once had he allowed any air between them. He was getting much too carried away with this newlywed game.

"Do you have plans for today?" he asked rather loudly. What did he have to do, clap like a seal to get her to even look at him?

"As a matter of fact, I'm planning to go around town and take some pictures." Kelsey kept her eyes on the water in the glass teakettle that she'd set on top of the stove to boil.

"I can take off another day and go with you. You don't know your way around." He was already knocking his head against a brick wall. He figured he could knock a little louder.

"I have a map of the subway system and a tour guide book. I'm perfectly capable of getting around on my own." She removed the tea bag from the box in the bread drawer, and a mug from the cabinet overhead.

"New York is not like London. You need to be more streetwise than you are to get around here."

"I'm streetwise," Kelsey responded aloofly.

Frankie expelled a vocal breath through his teeth, something Kelsey had seen him do before when he was annoyed.

"What's the point in going around asking for trouble?"

"I'm not going to get into trouble. I'll have you know that I've taken jujitsu lessons." One, to be exact. "I don't need a keeper."

She was really hostile this morning. "Do you want to tell me what you're mad about?" he asked, knowing.

"I'm not mad."

"Does this have something to do with my kissing you last night?"

Kelsey shot Frankie a withering glance. "I'm sure your girlfriend likes the way you kiss. Personally, I don't care for it."

"You don't like how I kiss?" Frankie muttered.

Cold-shouldering him, Kelsey poured water into her mug, dunked her tea bag and started for the table. "You roll your lips too much."

"I roll my lips too much," Frankie repeated tightly. He was getting hot under the collar, and the shirt he was wearing didn't even have a collar.

Kelsey sat across from him. "Why don't we not talk about it? I'm not all that interested in critiquing you."

"I'm interested in hearing it," Frankie retorted. "If my life gets any more interesting, I'm going to have to start selling tickets for tours."

Kelsey glared in response to his repartee. "You may think all your remarks are amusing. I don't."

Frankie ran his fingers through his hair, his coffee and cake forgotten. "Obviously not. My routine doesn't seem to have made a dent on you."

"No, it hasn't," Kelsey confirmed for him. He looked harmless, but he was actually toxic.

"Is there anything else about me you don't like? Go ahead. I'm wearing my bulletproof ego this morning."

Kelsey didn't like this conversation. "I'm sure there are things about me that you don't like...." Her voice trailed off. She didn't actually want to hear whatever it was, though she wouldn't have been surprised if he had a list. He was not bringing out the best in her.

Frankie tipped back in his chair and let out an exasperated breath. "You are something. I don't know what. But you are something."

Kelsey got up from the table. "I don't know what that means." She knew she didn't care for it just from his delivery."

"Come back here and have your tea," Frankie said sharply as Kelsey started to leave the kitchen.

She glared at him over her shoulder. "I don't want it anymore." However, she did come back to the table. She picked up her mug, brought it to the sink and washed it out.

Frankie rubbed his face in his hands. Thumbs hooked under his jaw, he steepled his fingers and blew into his palms. She was a workout....

At four-thirty that afternoon, Charlie Peterson just happened to be closest to the phone when it rang.

"Hello. Frankie's Bar and Grill," Charlie answered. Though the sign outside hadn't been changed yet, Billy had been bought out and Charlie considered the place to be all Frankie's.

"Charlie, is that you?" Kelsey asked intently on the other end.

"Kelsey? What's wrong? You don't sound right."

Frankie had been walking by. At Charlie's words he stopped in his tracks.

Kelsey swallowed hard. "I'm in jail.... Please don't tell Frankie. Just could you come here? Someone has to vouch for me and pay my fine so I can leave."

"I'll be right there. Tell me where you are? Wait a second. Let me get something to write it on." Frantically, Charlie motioned to Frankie.

Frankie handed Charlie paper and a pencil. While Charlie wrote nervously off slant, Frankie read over his shoulder. Frankie felt his heart start racing a mile a minute. Charlie was putting down the name and address of a police precinct in midtown.

Finally Charlie hung up. "She doesn't want you to know. I have to go there and get her out." Charlie hit himself in the head with his hand. "I forgot to ask her how much the fine was. Do you think they'll take a check?"

"I don't know, but I'll take cash and a business check with me," Frankie replied on his way out of the kitchen.

Charlie followed as Frankie went to the register behind the bar and just about cleaned out the till.

"She doesn't want you to go get her," Charlie said.

"She's my *wife*," Frankie stated firmly as he tore out a page of checks from his business checkbook and walked out the door.

"I told Charlie not to tell you," Kelsey grumbled while Frankie paid her two-hundred-dollar fine. She was mortified and worn out. The processing of her case had gone on for hours. Most of that time, she'd been in a holding cell along with a couple of women who practiced the oldest profession in the world. Immune to their own circumstances, and liking her accent, they'd tried to cheer her up. Any other time Kelsey would have loved to have taken their picture. They'd both had really interesting faces, and the jail-cell setting would have been a terrific backdrop... if she hadn't also been behind the bars and hadn't had her camera confiscated.

Frankie put an arm around Kelsey's shoulders while the desk officer wrote up a cash receipt. Unyielding as she was, Kelsey was no match for the force of Frankie's insistence. He got her close to his side.

The desk officer handed Kelsey her belongings—her camera and then her wallet in a plastic bag. Kelsey stuffed her wallet, plastic bag and all, into the back pocket of her jeans. "I had a map and a tour book," she said in a small voice.

"Don't see it here," the officer answered.

"I'll get you another map and tour book," Frankie said, then walked Kelsey across the reception hall of the precinct with its gray-washed walls and high ceilings. He couldn't wait to get her out of there.

Kelsey held her camera in her hand, its broken strap hanging to the floor. Hips brushing, Kelsey and Frankie descended the stone steps outside the door to the street. Kelsey shrugged out of Frankie's grasp. He let her go.

"They said you were in a fight." He studied her extensively. "Are you all right? Were you hurt? Bruised?"

"I'm not hurt." Kelsey didn't actually whimper, but she felt as if she might.

"Are you positive?" Frankie couldn't stop looking her over.

"I'm positive," she answered, her voice stronger.

"I parked just down the street. Wait here. I'll go get the car."

Kelsey shuddered at the thought of even standing in front of the precinct. "I'll go with you."

"I think what you need is a drink and some soul food." Frank spoke as they walked. "I'll take you to Little Italy."

At the mention of food, Kelsey realized how hungry she was. She hadn't gotten around to eating. "You don't have to take me to a restaurant. If you could just drive me back to your flat, I'll make something for myself."

"Could you quit being obstinate for a while and give us both a break?" He knew he sounded irritable. He wasn't irritable. He was shaken. She'd just scared the daylights out of him. "Please?" He softened his tone.

When he put his arm back around her shoulders, Kelsey didn't try to yank away. "Just say it," she said belligerently.

"I don't want to say it," he responded, spotting a phone booth. "Let's call your grandfather and let him know you're okay."

Shoulders slumped, Kelsey stood outside the open door of the phone booth while Frankie dialed.

"I have her. She's fine," Frankie said into the receiver when Charlie answered.

Kelsey accepted the phone when Frankie held it out to her. "I'm fine," she responded into the mouthpiece, feeling terrible at having upset Charlie. "Yes, really."

Frankie took the receiver back. "I'm going to take her for something to eat, and then home. Tell Eddie to close up for me tonight. Honestly, she's fine."

Frankie surveyed Kelsey as he hung up. Her eyes were downcast, but she seemed to be all right physically. He didn't think the same could be said about her emotional state of mind.

His car was parked just a bit down the block. Frankie slipped his arm around Kelsey's waist before he escorted her the rest of the way. She kept looking down at the camera in her hands. From what Frankie could tell, the lens appeared to be cracked.

"Do you want to tell me what happened?" Frankie asked after they were both in the car and he'd pulled onto the street.

"No." Kelsey stubbornly shook her head.

"How about just telling me where you were when it happened?"

"Forty-second Street."

Oh, no! Frankie thought to himself. "What in the world were you doing on Forty-second Street?" He was starting to get the picture. She'd probably been picked up by the vice squad.

"Taking shots of the way people relate to their surroundings, and the way surroundings relate to people. It's a very colorful area."

Was she nuts? "Did someone proposition you?" Is that what happened?" How could he have been stupid enough to let her go off on her own?

"No." Kelsey looked at him as if he'd said something lame. "I guess I took a picture of someone who didn't want their picture taken. This big ape of a guy came over to me and told me to take the roll of film out of my camera and give it to him. I told him no. He pulled the camera from me and he broke the strap right off my neck. So I kicked him."

Frankie turned his head away from Kelsey so that she wouldn't see him smile. "I don't suppose that I need to ask where you aimed?"

Kelsey shrugged. "I missed, but I did get him in the knee."

"What happened then?"

"He removed the roll of film and threw my camera on the ground. I think I jumped on his back at this point. The next thing I knew one of your policemen was there and he put handcuffs on me. He made me get into the back of his car. He said I was causing a public disturbance."

"No two ways about it, I'm going to have to track that big ape down and make mincemeat out of him for you," Frankie teased to insert some humor into her mood.

He made her smile. "I think you could overpower him, even though he's bigger than you are."

"Hold the phone," Frankie razzed. "Did you just give me a compliment?"

"I've noticed that you're fit." Kelsey didn't have to cogitate that appraisal.

"You have?" The gaze Frankie delivered had a hook to it. He was fishing. Since he was stopped in traffic he had plenty of time to reel it on out.

Kelsey turned her head aside. His teasing was one thing. His flirting was something else. "I'm sorry you had to take time off from the bar to come get me. I know how inconvenient it must be for you to have me around. I hope you're not staying entirely away from your girlfriend because of me."

It was on the tip of Frankie's tongue to alleviate that particular concern of hers, but something held him back. "I told you that she's okay about this situation, and so am I." That wasn't exactly a lie. "You know what they say. Absence makes the heart grow fonder."

Kelsey knew *she* wouldn't be okay about it if she was in Frankie's girlfriend's shoes.

"How much will a new lens cost?" Frankie asked, glancing at the camera she was cradling in her lap.

"I have others. This was just my favorite one."

"I would like to see some of your photos."

"You would?"

"Uh-huh," Frankie answered.

"All right. When we get home." It startled Kelsey how easily the word *home* had come out of her mouth. She didn't actually think of his flat as her home, though it was her home temporarily.

"I really appreciate your coming to get me out of jail. I'll pay you back the money for my fine. If there's any time that I can do something for you, just ask."

It was a perfect opening for Frankie to reply with an innuendo. He squelched that instinct. "There is a way you could help me. I'm having a hell of a time trying to figure out what to do to redecorate the bar. Would you consider giving me some ideas?"

"Absolutely, only I haven't had any schooling in decorating." Kelsey was excited by the prospect.

"You're creative. That's something I know that I'm not." Frankie put his hand out—just wanting to touch her.

Kelsey placed both her hands in her lap and squared herself in her seat. "Is this Little Italy?" She would have liked holding hands with him. That feeling made her even more unsettled than she already was.

"This is it," Frankie verified, covering up that he was chafed at her brush-off. "Watch for a parking space on your side. The restaurant we're going to is just a block away."

Kelsey had a sudden scary thought. "Do you think immigration will find out that I was arrested? What if I've killed my chance of getting a green card?"

"You don't have a record. You haven't killed your chance of getting a green card." The only thing she'd killed off was the show of affection he'd attempted to give her.

Later that evening Frankie sat on the living room couch and looked through the albums of photos that Kelsey had brought with her from London. He'd felt restless during dinner and hadn't eaten much. His disposition was much the same now, though he was very impressed by what he was looking at.

Kelsey rambled around the living room. Her stomach was doing flips as she awaited his opinion. She was glad she hadn't eaten all that much.

Frankie picked up the third and last book. His eyes moved to Kelsey. She was turned away from him, bent at the waist to look at his cassette tape collection. His gaze latched onto the part of her body that was pointed in his direction.

Frankie dragged in a frustrated breath, trying to douse the thoughts that came into his head. "Put something on if you like." She was right. He was a cad.

With a start, Kelsey turned at Frankie's voice. "You seem to like jazz," she said.

"Yes," Frankie replied, opening the last photo album. He had to remind himself that she might be his wife, but first and foremost she was Charlie's granddaughter. And he owed Charlie a lot—including his trust.

Kelsey selected a tape at random. It was all brass, plus lots of throbbing saxophones. Kelsey listened to the music while she walked around and cast glances at Frankie. His hair was falling over his forehead while he concentrated on her work.

Frankie felt his mouth go dry as he came upon a picture of Kelsey. She was wearing shorts and a half shirt that left her midriff exposed. Sprawled on a sofa with her legs propped over one side and her ankles crossed, she was holding a kitten over her head. Was her skin really that creamy? Or was it just the lighting?

"Good or bad?" Kelsey asked apprehensively, having watched him linger long on one particular page.

"Good," Frankie answered thickly, and quickly flipped to the next photo.

Kelsey saw Frankie rake his hair back from his forehead and wondered what it would feel like if she were to do that for him. Digging her hands into the back pockets of her jeans, she resumed her stroll around the room.

Frankie closed the book and put it down on the coffee table on top of the other two. Kelsey stopped walking.

"Would you be interested in selling some of these to me?" Frankie smiled at the way Kelsey's eyes widened.

"You really want to buy some?" Kelsey could hardly believe it.

Frankie nodded his head.

"Are you just saying that?"

"I could just say they're terrific. I'm putting my money where my mouth is."

"Which ones?" There was still a hint of suspicion in Kelsey's gaze as she moseyed on over to him. It was possible that he was just trying to make her feel better because she'd been in jail.

Frankie gestured with his chin to the cushion at his side. "Sit down and I'll show you."

"I wasn't very nice to you this morning," Kelsey said, not sitting quite as near to him as she'd first seemed set to do.

Frankie grinned. "Are you apologizing?"

"Yes."

"Because I want to buy some of your photos?" He was only half-teasing.

"Oh... This does sound that way." Kelsey's eyes lowered. Frankie felt it was forever before they came up to him again. "Honestly," Kelsey said. "I know I owe you an apology."

"I accept." Frankie held on to her gaze. "Just for the record, are you apologizing for your attitude or your remarks?"

"Are you referring to the remark about by not liking the way you kiss?" Her expression was teasing.

"That's the remark." Keep it light, Frankie warned himself.

"I lied. I don't really think you roll your lips too much." Kelsey pushed her hair behind her ears and pulled her eyes off Frankie's mouth. "Could we talk about my photos?"

"Do you need time to think about pricing them?"

"You can just say you like them. You don't have to buy them. Don't take this wrong, but I know that money isn't that important to you."

"Are you kidding?" Frankie contradicted. "I'm out to make as much as I can to prove myself."

"That's different." Kelsey got to her feet and started walking around again. "Would you take ten photos in exchange for paying my jail fine?"

"You'd be selling yourself short." Frankie sensed she was about to take flight.

Kelsey took a step toward the bedroom, then asked, "What are you going to do with the photos?"

"Frame them and hang them up at the bar."

"That's one of the nicest things anyone has ever said to me."

"I have my moments," Frankie replied, and wanted to come up with something more to say to keep her in the room. "Is tomorrow convenient for you to come into the bar and give me some ideas?"

"Tomorrow is fine. Well..." Kelsey dawdled a second. "I guess I'll say good-night."

"Good night, Kelsey."

Kelsey stopped at the bedroom door. "About this morning... Thanks for wanting to look out for me."

Frankie nodded. "That's what husbands are for."

Chapter Seven

"Have I met everyone that works for you?" Kelsey asked as Frankie pulled away from the curb. They'd just come out of an art supply store and were now on their way to the bar.

"My cousin Cosmo hasn't been in when you've been around. He's my accountant."

"Did I meet your cousin Cosmo at the party?"

"Yes." Frankie wagged his eyebrows up and down. If he had to stuff a fist in his mouth, he was going to keep the harmony going between them. "He's the one who looks like gloom and doom. I keep a box of antacid behind the bar, and I pop them down when he shows up."

"If he upsets you, why don't you just use another accountant?"

"And take business away from the family?" Frankie sent Kelsey a slow smile. "We're very close-knit, in case you haven't noticed. My cousin Cosmo does the books for everyone who has a business in the family. He shares tax season with cousin Lou. He was also at the party—tall, thin, good-looking guy...Lou Figliozzi. Lou has been coming around quite a bit lately. He's got his eye on Esther."

Kelsey didn't remember one cousin's face from any of the other. "I suppose you have lawyers and doctors in the family, as well."

"Of course. We've got just about everything covered. If you need something, there's someone in the family who can do it for you, or get it for you, usually wholesale."

"But you don't have any interior decorators in the family?"

"No." Frankie kept his sexy eyes on her for so long that Kelsey considered they might get into an accident. "I've got to tell you, when the word gets out, you'll be swamped."

It hit Kelsey as Frankie put his full attention back on his driving that the chances of her being in the family long enough for that to happen were slim to nil. "You're very lucky to have a large family."

"Yes." Frankie was positive he knew what was going on in her head. He heard the ache she was trying to keep out of her voice. "I thought your mother would want to make a trip over here once you told her you'd gotten married."

"She does. She hasn't said it but I think the idea of meeting Charlie is holding her back."

To Frankie's surprise, he considered getting in touch with her mother himself. He figured, as Kelsey probably did, that if her mother came and met Charlie they'd find the ties that bind.

"Did I see a picture of your mother in your albums?" He'd selected ten pictures as she'd suggested in exchange for her jail fine. He thought of the picture of her that he hadn't included in the barter—how he'd looked at it again after she'd left the living room.

"No, but I do have a number of photos of her. I gave Charlie a few when he asked me for some." She was still mixed-up about what she should feel toward Charlie. She was even more mixed-up about what she should feel toward her make-believe husband.

"Will you come with me when I go to get frames for mine? I'm sure you'll know better than I will what looks right."

"I've never had my work hung up in public. Are you certain—"

"I'm certain," Frankie cut in with a smile. "In fact, I'm going to put a plaque up saying the work of Kelsey—"

This time Kelsey cut Frankie off. "No plaque." It would have been ridiculous for him to say Falco.

"Okay. No plaque." He'd almost blown it.

Kelsey didn't feel like talking anymore. Frankie just drove.

Eddie Rodriguez, who helped Frankie to manage the place, was the first to greet Kelsey. He was a handsome man—smooth face, dark curly hair, prankish brown eyes, early thirties. Eddie gave Frankie a locker-room wink. "If I'd met her eight months ago, I would have given you a run for the money."

Kelsey smiled a greeting, taking Eddie's comment for what it was—a friendly gesture. Kelsey could tell that Frankie and Eddie got along very well. They were cut from the same cloth.

Frankie grinned. "My mother didn't raise any stupid kids, even if I'm the runt of the litter."

Kelsey knew Frankie had meant the last of his remark to be joking, but it spoke of his inner sensitivity. Kelsey wanted to tell Frankie that she believed in him. He was going to make a success of this place and himself.

Kelsey gave the surroundings her full regard. Frankie's bar did need a new personality. Sports memorabilia hung on walls that were putty colored from the middle up, and wood paneled from the middle down. The bar itself had to be about twenty feet long. The dark wood was heavily polished, but it still had a tortured appearance, as did the laminated wood tables and chairs.

The ceiling was great, Kelsey decided, looking up. It was made of old-fashioned stamped metal and had an air of vintage charm. She had the same good feeling about the hanging fixtures, which might have been up since the place was first built.

Charlie came up front from the kitchen, a corner of his white apron at his eyes. He'd been chopping onions.

Charlie looked as awkward as Kelsey when they first saw each other. "Frankie called and said he was bringing you in to give him some decorating ideas."

"I'm going to try my best," Kelsey answered, hanging back when what she was sorely tempted to do was greet him with an embrace. For all the times they'd been together now she was still unsettled about how to connect. It felt to Kelsey like being in a marching band, starting off on the wrong foot and not being able to get in step.

Frankie tried to mentally telegraph a message to Charlie. Give her a hug. Take a chance. She needs a hug.

"Where's everyone?" Suzie, one of the bar's two waitresses, called out from the kitchen, having walked in through the back door.

"We're up front," Frankie answered.

Suzie passed by the open window to the kitchen and then through the swing door. She came toward them in a white blouse and short skirt, holding her uniform on a hanger over her shoulder. She was blond, blue eyed, trim and pretty.

The waitress did something Kelsey wished she felt free to do. She affectionately gave Charlie a quick squeeze. "Thank goodness she doesn't take after you," Suzie ribbed Charlie as she smiled a hello to Kelsey.

Kelsey smiled back.

"I'm so glad you came in," Suzie said warmly. "Keep me company while I get changed. We can get acquainted before the boss and his other half start cracking a whip." The waitress passed a saucy look between Frankie and Eddie.

"A whip, huh?" Eddie took up the game. "Why haven't you told me that's what I needed to get somewhere with you?"

Esther interrupted Suzie and Eddie's playtime, coming through the kitchen right then.

"Hi, everyone." Esther, the bar's other waitress, bustled over. Like Suzie, she was carrying her uniform on a hanger. Her dark hair was caught to one side with a rubber band. She had on a loose-fitting shirt over jersey jogging pants. Kelsey didn't indulge herself in the knowledge that she measured up in appearance to either of these two women.

"Kelsey is going to keep us company while we get dressed," Suzie told Esther.

Kelsey looked to Frankie. "I'll hold on to those for you," he said, taking a sketch pad and pencils from her hand.

Suzie led the way, with Kelsey and Esther bringing up the rear.

Charlie went back to the kitchen. Eddie walked to the bar to finish taking inventory. Frankie stood where he was and watched Kelsey walk away.

Eddie whistled goadingly to Frankie when the door to the dressing room closed. "I thought that once you get married you're not supposed to have it that bad."

Frankie gave an exaggerated shrug, and pretended to be busy.

"How's married life?" Esther asked Kelsey companionably as she changed into her uniform.

"It's been wonderful," Kelsey responded appropriately.

"I'm so glad he didn't wind up with—" Suzie stopped midsentence as Esther threw her a warming glance.

Kelsey wanted to put both women at ease. "I know he'd been seeing someone else." He's still attached to her, Kelsey could have added. Naturally, she didn't.

"He's a great guy," Esther said.

"He really is," Suzie seconded. "He'll be better off here not having a partner. The one he had wasn't giving this business the attention it needs. This place can do a lot better than it's been doing."

Esther stepped into her uniform. "I'm glad you came around. A woman should take an active interest in her husband's business."

"I don't have much of a business mind," Kelsey answered. "I'm here to hopefully give Frankie some decorating ideas."

Suzie, now in her uniform, looked at Esther. "Es, we should tell her."

"Tell me what?" Kelsey felt a quickening of her pulse.

"Monica has come in a couple of times," Esther divulged, arriving at the decision that if she were Kelsey, she'd want to be told. "They spoke together. That's all. Frankie didn't go anywhere with her. I hope she shows up when you're here. That should straighten her out."

Kelsey hadn't known Frankie's girlfriend's name. Now she did. Kelsey supposed that she should feel pleased that at the very least Frankie and Monica were spending a little time with each other. Only she couldn't have said that she felt pleased.

"I expect that they're still friends," Kelsey responded thinly.

"Frankie didn't look like he was encouraging her," Suzie said, not wanting Kelsey to worry.

Kelsey thought to herself that Frankie must have been concerned that Charlie wouldn't approve of his girlfriend coming around.

"What is she like?" Kelsey was irked with herself for asking.

"Every woman's nightmare," Suzie sneered.

Kelsey definitely did not want to see Frankie and Monica together!

"Unbelievably self-centered," Esther elaborated. "Monica is the kind of woman who stays home if she's having a bad hair day."

"I hope all her hair falls out," Kelsey blurted, and couldn't believe what she'd said.

Esther laughed. "Just keep in mind that Frankie had plenty of time to propose to her and he didn't. He's crazy about you, Kelsey. You've got him walking around in a daze."

"I'm in a daze myself," Kelsey responded. What could be crazier than the arrangement they'd put themselves in?

"We'd better get out of here before Eddie comes banging the door down." Suzie gave her blond hair a flick of her fingers.

"When are you going to give that guy a break and let him take you out?" Esther asked Suzie as they all left the dressing room.

"Eddie's getting close," Suzie responded to Esther. "Don't you dare tell him. I like the chase."

As soon as Kelsey came down the hallway with Esther and Suzie, Frankie walked out from behind the bar, where he'd been talking to Eddie. Esther and Suzie took off to get started.

"Let's sit down and I'll tell you what my thinking is for the place," Frankie said, coming up to Kelsey.

Kelsey sat in the chair he held out for her. She breathed in his after-shave. He'd showered right before she had this morning after they'd cleaned the apartment, though as their bathroom schedule went, he'd also showered the night before. Kelsey thought about how she'd used the soap he'd used still lathered from his skin, though she did have her own personal soap in the bathroom, covered in a plastic container. She'd used his washcloth, as well.

"You're the first one I'm discussing this with." Seated across from her, Frankie rapped his fingers on the top of the table. Kelsey was instantly aware that he was tense.

"I've decided to turn the place into a jazz club," Frankie went on. "Not just a nightclub. I want to run the place for a lunchtime crowd and dinnertime crowd, as well. I'm trying to cover all my bases. Jazz and good home cooking."

Kelsey was thrilled to be the first one he was discussing his idea with. It sounded great to her, which was exactly what she told him.

"You really think so." Frankie gave her a lingering smile. "You wouldn't just be saying it?"

"No," Kelsey answered, doing her best to show him her sincerity.

Frankie relaxed. "The decorating end is probably going to be a problem. The budget is limited."

"The ceiling and fixtures are great for your idea." She overrode what she could of his concern. "All they need is some heavy-duty cleaning and polishing to bring them back to life."

"I want a piano player during the day and a combo at night with a blues singer...that kind of thing. I was worried at first about the cost of entertainment, but then I thought Uncle Vinnie—"

"Uncle Vinnie sings the blues?" If he did, Kelsey couldn't picture it. Opera, maybe. He did have an operatic build.

Frankie laughed, getting the same image in his mind as Kelsey had in hers. "No, but Uncle Vinnie is always in touch with untapped talent. There's got to be plenty of musicians that haven't been discovered yet who would like a place to showcase their stuff. If Uncle Vinnie can't come up with anyone, Teddy might be able to. Did I tell you Teddy is a rock-and-roll promoter?"

Kelsey shook her head and then her eyebrows puckered together. "Frankie, if you don't like the decorating ideas I come up with I don't want you to be concerned about hurting my feelings."

"Hey." Frankie reached across and squeezed Kelsey's hand. "We're a team. The dream team. We'll talk our ideas through. We'll arrive at the same place.

Suzie stepped up to their table and bantered, "The two of you are starting to embarrass the rest of us. Are you both going to sit around mooning over each other all day?"

"That's a thought." Frankie gave Kelsey a risqué wink.

It was only an act, Kelsey said to herself, even if it felt like the real thing. She came right back at him with an equally irreverent look.

Suzie walked off laughing.

Frankie kept the devilry in his dark brown eyes. "We seem to have gotten the hang of this."

Getting in over their heads was more like it. "I'm going to do some work now," Kelsey said, standing.

It was getting busy. Frankie could see that as he watched Kelsey flip open her sketch pad and walk around the room. He went back to work behind the bar.

When the lunch crowd thinned and he got a breather, Frankie scanned the place for Kelsey. It took him a second to find her. She was standing talking to some male who was looking over her shoulder at her sketch pad. He couldn't hear what she was saying, he could only see that her mouth was moving and the pencil in her hand was still. There was a look on her face that he was having trouble reading. It wasn't until he cut to the guy with his head angled toward her that he figured it out.

"I said I wasn't interested," Kelsey repeated in a measured voice.

"If you've had your lunch, get out." Frankie spoke, coming up behind Kelsey. "If you haven't had your lunch, the kitchen just closed."

"You can't just throw a customer out," the man replied. He was in his twenties, tight jeans, black T-shirt pushed up to show off well-developed biceps.

"Watch me," Frankie threatened.

The two men visually accosted each other.

"What's the problem, anyway?" the slightly younger one asked.

"The problem is that you've been coming on to my wife. I can tell you, pal, I don't appreciate it."

Kelsey glanced from Frankie to his customer and then back to Frankie. She knew that if she was really Frankie's wife she would have been thrilled with his show of possessiveness. But she wasn't really his wife.

She was only married to him. He was a cad to make her even consider feeling cherished.

"Hey, man, I don't go after the ones that are taken. If I were you, I'd put a wedding band on her finger."

"I lost it yesterday," Kelsey said stiffly as Frankie's eyes went to her left hand.

"This is the last time I come in here," the bane of Frankie's irritation said on his way to the front door.

Frankie motioned to Eddie, who was behind the bar. Eddie came over. "Hold the fort down. Kelsey and I will be back in a little while."

"Where are we going?" Kelsey asked as Frankie towed her out the door.

"There's a jewelry store just down the street."

"I could have handled that situation myself," Kelsey said querulously. "I didn't need you to intercede for me."

"I know. You're real tough." She was testing his patience.

"You are not my protector!"

"Fine! I'm not your protector, and I'm not your keeper. But I am your husband."

"You're not even that," Kelsey fired back.

"You're not much of a wife, either, but you are going to damn well wear a wedding band."

"If I'm going to wear one, then you can just damn well wear one, too."

Chapter Eight

Agitated, Kelsey turned to the next recipe in the gourmet cookbook she'd bought the day before. They were all complicated. The last one asked for liquid smoke. What the devil was that? And what did it have to do with sweet-and-sour leg of lamb? Kelsey couldn't imagine how she'd never before thought about the fact the leg of lamb was some poor lamb's leg.

Frankie stirred. Half awake, half asleep, he opened the lid of one eye to check the time on his watch. It was 6:00 a.m. Even if he had to open the bar, he would have had plenty of time. Only he didn't have to open the bar. He'd been closed for two days now for renovations and the contractors had their own key. Anyway, it was Sunday.

Kelsey closed the hardcover cookbook with a slam. She reached for her third cup of tea. In the process, she knocked the book over with her elbow. It hit the brown-and-white-checkered linoleum floor.

Frankie opened both his eyes at the bang. Raising his head off the pillow, he looked into the kitchen from the convertible couch. He didn't see all of Kelsey, just her crossed pajama legs under the table. She was swinging her upper leg back and forth.

He thought about the ideas that she'd come up with for the bar that were now incorporated into the blueprints. They'd spent two weeks working together with measuring tapes, checking out wholesalers, going over paint chips and fabrics—surrounding themselves with samples. They'd debated. They'd discussed. He'd discovered that he had no color sense at all, but she did.

Inhaling deeply, Kelsey bent and picked the cookbook up from the floor. She opened it randomly and began searching through it again.

Frankie rubbed his face, got up and walked into the kitchen doorway. "I don't know why you're making yourself a nervous wreck over your mother's visit."

Kelsey sent Frankie an exasperated look. "If you don't want to support my nervousness, then be neutral. Those are the choices for today."

Frankie suppressed a grin. "Can I decide which way I want to go after I have my coffee?"

"Could you please put some clothes on first?" Kelsey was finding it impossible to keep her eyes off his bare chest, and her mind was already complicated enough.

"Give me a break." Frankie's smile escaped. "These are outdoor shorts."

Kelsey pointed to his top half. "The kitchen is not the seashore."

"I'll get a shirt." Frankie started to turn, but stopped to tease. "I don't turn you on, do I?"

"Hardly." Kelsey crossed her fingers under the table. She'd been having very sexy thoughts about him. She could even pinpoint exactly when they'd begun. They'd started the day she'd taken her shower with his soap.

Frankie went into the bathroom to wash. Kelsey put up a pot of coffee for him, and put some more water up to boil for herself.

"Have you decided on a recipe?" Frankie called from the living room a short while later. He'd washed and brushed his teeth, deciding to leave off shaving for now.

"Not yet," Kelsey answered. "Would you like some eggs this morning?"

"Sounds good," Frankie said, coming back into the kitchen, pulling a shirt over his head. "I love the way you make eggs. How's that for support?"

"Omelets are the only thing I cook well."

Frankie took out the container of orange juice from the fridge. "Why don't you just make omelets for dinner? You can stuff them with something."

"I am not going to serve my mother and Charlie omelets." Kelsey struck a flabbergasted pose.

"I'm sure if you ask Charlie he'd be glad to do the cooking and bring it over before he goes to pick up your mother." He could see in her eyes that he had pushed the wrong button.

"My mother said to me once that cooking a special meal for someone was a way of showing how much you care."

Frankie got it then. She wasn't just cooking a meal. She was trying to show the two most important people in her life how much she cared. Without a doubt, he could be a jerk sometimes.

He watched her go to the refrigerator for butter and eggs. It was the first time he'd seen her in pajamas without a robe over them. He knew she was too flustered to give a thought to her appearance. The sight of her like this made Frankie almost forget that they were just pretending to be a married couple. Of course, having just woken up in bed alone was certainly a reminder.

The coffee stopped dripping and the teakettle started to whistle almost simultaneously. Frankie poured himself a cup of coffee, and fixed Kelsey a fresh cup of tea.

"If they were coming for lunch I could have done tea sandwiches," Kelsey said, thinking out loud as she beat two eggs into a froth. "I'm pretty good with tea sandwiches. I've even invented some combinations."

"What, pray tell, is a tea sandwich?" Frankie asked, his hip parked against the counter, sipping his coffee. He studied the way the yellow cotton fabric of her pajama top followed the untethered contour of her breasts.

"Usually it's butter with watercress. Cream cheese with thinly sliced cucumbers. Cream cheese with a bit of chives. White bread. No crusts." Kelsey spread butter onto the frying pan as she set it to heat. "I've done them with kippers, truffles and anchovies."

"You've lost me on the kippers and truffles, but anchovies I know." She'd never cooked anything for him but breakfast, Frankie contemplated, though he was always the one suggesting they bring home take-out food when they hadn't been at the bar going over sketches, bouncing suggestions back and forth. On the nights they'd eaten at home, they'd had pizza and Chinese food. Would she have even thought to cook something special for him if he'd given her the green light?

Frankie turned to the kitchen window and looked out on the city awakening in a flood of sunlight. "I could go to the store later and get you some fixings for tea sandwiches. We could have them for lunch."

"I can get some fixings." Kelsey poured the eggs into the frying pan. "I'll be going to the store anyway to buy what I'll need to cook dinner."

Frankie took another swallow of his coffee before going to the refrigerator for a loaf of white bread. Nutty as it was, he felt pleased that he'd graduated from breakfast to lunch.

Kelsey worked a fork around the sides of the pan to keep the omelet she was making from sticking. "Did you ever realize how different meat sounds when you think about it raw, instead of cooked?"

"I haven't thought about it." Standing next to her again, Frankie put four slices of white bread into the toaster. He didn't think she'd had her toast yet. Two slices of toast was the most she ever ate in the morning. She'd spread them heavily with butter and orange marmalade. He'd tasted the stuff. It wasn't half-bad.

Kelsey slid the omelet from the pan onto a plate. "I am fabulous with eggs," she said, pleased with herself.

Frankie couldn't help ribbing her. "And modest, too."

"No wisecracks until I settle dinner in my mind," Kelsey countered.

"Okay." Frankie raised his hands in surrender before he took the plate from her. He was having a hard time keeping his appetite confined to food. Her hair was begging for his fingers. She hadn't combed it yet and it waved errantly around her shiny, unmade-up face. He was trying to keep his eyes from straying below her neck.

"By the way, I do know how to cook," he told her.

"You know how to cook?" Kelsey queried in surprised.

The toast popped. Frankie put it on another plate and started for the table. "Don't you think the male ego can be domesticated?"

"I do believe in equality of the sexes."

Frankie grinned. "Believe me, you've made that very clear." He held up his left hand with the wedding band on his finger. He'd gotten used to the feel.

Kelsey smiled smartly. "How did you learn to cook?"

"It's hard not to learn something about cooking growing up in an Italian household. My mother reared us in the kitchen."

Kelsey pondered an image of him as a young boy as she brought his coffee and her tea to the table. Full of mischief, she suspected, as she went to the drawer for silverware. What had his mother called him? She remembered only that it was the Italian word for tease.

"Why do you think your mother decided to let Charlie meet her plane and show her to her hotel?" Frankie asked from his seat at the table.

"It was all the old letters," Kelsey answered, sitting across from him, buttering a slice of toast for herself. "My mother found them when she cleaned out the attic in my grandmother's house, now that the house has finally been sold." Kelsey passed Frankie the butter. In many ways he was becoming her confidant.

"What letters?"

"Letters that Charlie wrote to my mother that my grandmother never let her see. I expect that my grandmother worried that my mother might love her less if she loved Charlie, as well. It's sad."

Frankie nodded. He hadn't had the chance to contact her mother himself and was glad the woman was coming to visit of her own volition.

Kelsey regarded Frankie as he spread butter on his toast. She knew he would put some of the omelet she'd made him on the bread next and eat it that way. She was becoming very familiar with his habits; she even knew when to expect his smile. She knew his entire wardrobe and the way he always sat on the edge of the couch when he watched a sports event on the telly. They'd rented videos last night and watched them in the living room. He'd made teasingly snide remarks through the romantic movie she'd picked out, and kidded her mercilessly every time she closed her eyes through the scary movie he'd selected.

Frankie finished off one slice of toast topped by half his omelet. "I'd be happy to help you with dinner."

Kelsey wanted to accept. "I'd rather do this on my own," she said instead. She couldn't very well allow herself to keep bonding with him. Lately that seemed to be happening to her with regularity. The line between fantasy and reality was almost a blur.

Frankie shrugged, annoyed at the way she always separated herself as soon as they seemed to be getting particularly close. "Whatever you want."

Kelsey finished her tea, ignoring the rest of her toast. Woodenly she went to the stove for the frying pan to scrub it clean. She knew he was irritated.

"Are you still planning to have your mother go on thinking that our marriage is real?" Frankie asked coolly.

"Yes. She has enough to concern herself with right now just meeting Charlie." Stressing, Kelsey accidentally splashed water on herself at the sink. It was then that she realized she hadn't put her robe on. She had not expected Frankie to wake as early as he had.

"I'll be right back," she told him, shutting off the faucet and turning toward the bedroom.

Frankie caught a look at the front of her pajama top, damp and clinging to her breasts. He stuffed his mouth with more toast.

Kelsey came back into the kitchen within a matter of minutes in shorts and a shirt buttoned down the front, tails hanging. "Do you have plans for today?" she asked, retracing her steps to the sink.

"No, but if you'd like me to do a disappearing act I will." He spoke to her back. Having lunch with her when she had her barriers up was no longer appealing.

"This is your flat. I wouldn't dream of putting you out," Kelsey responded over her shoulder, scrubbing the frying pan more than it needed to be scrubbed.

"I'll give my brother-in-law Sonny a call. If he's not on duty today, I'm sure I can talk him into a game of handball," Frankie answered matter-of-factly.

Kelsey attended to the spatula next. "I thought you mentioned last night that there was a baseball game that you wanted to see on the telly this afternoon."

Frankie almost asked if it would be all right with her. He would have said it sarcastically. "I'm going to shave," he replied instead, without any punctuation. "I'll straighten the living room up before I leave."

Using his key, Frankie let himself back into his apartment at five o'clock. He'd watched the baseball game at Sonny and Angie's place. He'd never before not enjoyed seeing the way marriage agreed with the two of them. Today, however, he'd left feeling low, antsy, possibly envious. Strange feelings for him, given that marriage wasn't part of either his short- or long-range plans. He didn't exactly see himself being with only one woman for the rest of his life. Chances were, he wouldn't be all that good at marriage, anyway. He certainly wasn't scoring points in the one he was co-starring in.

Kelsey let out a yelp as she burned her hand grabbing a pot from the stove.

Like a madman, Frankie raced for the kitchen. "Are you all right?" He practically jumped her.

Kelsey bounced in place, holding one hand in the other. Her lips were clamped together. There was a grimace on her face.

Frankie didn't need her to answer. Taking both her hands in just one of his, he moved her over to the sink. He turned on the cold water and put her hands under the spray.

"I have some ointment in the bathroom. Keep your hand under the water," he instructed, then left to get the medication.

Kelsey gazed gloomily around the kitchen while the water ran over her hurt palm and through her fingers. She'd made a mess, and she hadn't even completed her preparations. On top of that, given the late hour, she was hardly going to have time to make herself presentable. Her mother and Charlie were due to arrive around seven. She'd wanted everything to be perfect.

Frankie came back. He turned off the water and dried Kelsey's hand with a clean dish towel. Examining her palm, he gently spread around the ointment. He could tell the skin was going to blister, and carefully put three Band-Aids in a row over the cream.

Deflated, Kelsey went to the table and sat in a chair. She held her injured hand out in front of her. "Thank you." Kelsey bit her bottom lip to prevent an outburst of tears.

Frankie wet the corner of the dish towel with cold water. He came over, hunkered down in front of her and wiped her heated face. He put the towel down and finger combed her tangled hair behind her ears. "You have just been elevated to a management position," he said, smiling softly.

"What do you mean?" She was worn-out, but very happy that he was back. She hadn't wanted him to leave her alone in the first place. She'd wanted him to stay, even if it was in another room.

"I mean that you give the orders and I'll finish up." He gave her a stern look. "Let me warn you, if you give me any of your back talk your bottom is going to be hurting as much as your hand." They both knew he would never lay a hand on her—except to make love to her—but it was hard to resist teasing her.

His teasing brought her a second wind. "I don't think I'd care to stand through dinner."

It was innocent repartee, but it brought physical pictures into both their minds. Avoiding another straight look at her, Frankie went for the recipe book opened on the counter. Kelsey examined the Band-Aids on her hand. Her breathing seemed amplified to her ears.

"I still can't get over how delicious everything was." Phoebe Shepherd smiled at her daughter. "When did you learn to cook like this?"

"It was Frankie—" Kelsey began, but Frankie overruled her.

"We did it together, Mrs. Shepherd," Frankie answered, fascinated as he'd been from the start at how much Kelsey took after her mother in appearance, except that the color of Kelsey's incredible eyes was different. Was that what she had taken from her father?

"Please make it Phoebe. You are my son-in-law."

"The two of you are putting me to shame," Charlie said.

To Kelsey, it seemed that her mother and grandfather were beginning to speak naturally. They didn't appear as uptight as when they'd first arrived. Kelsey hoped that the reunion would finally bring them together.

"Do the two of you eat like this every night?" Phoebe asked.

They'd just finished an entrée of chicken smothered in a white wine and sour cream sauce, along with scalloped potatoes and a medley of fresh string beans, carrots and zucchini.

"Not yet," Frankie answered. "We're still in the learning-to-just-live-with-each-other stage. There have been times that your daughter has looked like she'd prefer carving me up to a roast."

Phoebe laughed brightly. Charlie joined her.

Kelsey lightly punched Frankie's arm with her unbandaged hand. Theatrically, she bantered a phrase she'd heard him use. "Actually, that's a good call."

Frankie grinned, making Kelsey grin in return. She knew he liked it when she took his words and said them with her accent. Kelsey wondered if she might not try cooking him a gourmet meal one night, now that she'd figured out a recipe.

"So this is your first visit to the States," Frankie remarked. He knew any long pause in the table conversation was hard on Kelsey, Charlie and Phoebe.

"I thought I could show you some of the sights of the city tomorrow." Charlie looked hopefully at his daughter.

"We could all go around," Kelsey offered.

"Not tomorrow, sweetheart." Frankie interceded. "I told the contractor we'd meet him at the bar so that we could okay the last changes on the blueprints. You know, the ones you asked for."

She hadn't asked for a change to the blueprints.... Suddenly, though, Kelsey understood why he'd just said that. He was trying to give Charlie and her mother the opportunity of spending the day alone, getting to know each other.

"Yes, of course." Kelsey nodded, while her heart raced at how smart he was.

"Why don't we all plan to meet for dinner?" Frankie suggested. "Charlie and I will take you ladies out for a night on the town."

"That sounds lovely," Phoebe agreed, then sighed. "Darling, I hope you won't mind if I leave to go to my hotel now. I'm really quite tired."

"Mum, of course I don't mind. You must be exhausted."

They all pushed back their seats and got to their feet.

Phoebe regarded her father. "Charlie, you needn't end your evening. Is it possible to call for a taxi?"

"I will bring you back to your hotel," Charlie responded insistently. "We can decide on the way what sights you'd like to see tomorrow."

"All right." Phoebe offered her father a timid but personal smile.

Kelsey and Frankie walked the older couple out of the kitchen. Frankie had slipped his arm around Kelsey's waist, and Kelsey couldn't help thinking how perfectly right it felt.

At the front door Kelsey gave her mother a big hug and then spontaneously placed a shy kiss on her grandfather's cheek. When she straightened, Kelsey thought she spied tears at the corners of Charlie's eyes.

Frankie reached out and opened the door. Phoebe said, "Good night."

Charlie cleared his throat and said, "We'll see you both tomorrow. I'll call during the day and set a time for dinner."

As soon as Frankie closed the door Kelsey did a little jig and hop along the lines of a sports player who had just scored. "Don't you think that went well?" she asked, her eyes all glittery.

"That definitely went well." Frankie grinned, joining her high.

"You were wonderful."

He didn't see himself as having done anything to warrant her praise, but he wasn't about to dissuade her. "You," he said, pointing his finger at her, "are gorgeous."

"Thank you . . . thank you," Kelsey replied, soaring at his compliment, though she didn't agree with it. "You were absolutely charming. My mother liked you. You have a way with women."

Frankie had to keep a groan from surfacing. The one woman he wanted to have his way with was standing right in front of him—driving him to distraction at the moment. "How's your hand?"

"It's fine. I could take the bandages off right now if I didn't hate taking bandages off."

Frankie reached out and grabbed the wrist of the hand in question.

"Oh, no," Kelsey wailed, pushing at his chest.

Frankie leaned back against the wall, spreading his feet to make room for her. "I won't hurt you. I promise. Close your eyes."

"No." Kelsey shook her head adamantly. "Frankie, don't. Okay? It will come off in the shower some day."

He let go of her hand and tweaked her nose with his fingers. "Baby," he taunted, smiling.

Using both hands, Kelsey wildly messed up his hair in retribution.

Frankie raised an eyebrow, getting cocky with her. "Is that your best retaliation?"

Trying not to grin, Kelsey squared off with him. "It depends on what you're going to do back."

He did what he'd been wanting to do since the last time he'd done it. He put a proprietary arm around her waist and laid a fast, reckless kiss on her mouth, pulling her toward him.

"Your turn," he said, challenging her. Only it wasn't a game anymore, and they both knew it.

Slowly Kelsey wrapped her arms around Frankie's neck and put her lips against his.

As Frankie made the kiss deeper, he did consider for a second that he was taking advantage of her mood. But playing fair was the farthest thing from his mind as his hand slid to her rib cage. But as that hand slipped between them to cup her breast, her mouth stilled on his mouth.

Reluctantly Frankie ended the kiss and moved his wandering hand away.

"I guess we'd better stop," he said, his heart banging in his chest.

Kelsey started to turn away, stopped and turned back. She couldn't fight this. She ached to be with him. She was in love with him.

"Kelsey?" Frankie whispered. His voice was guttural and strained.

Kelsey flattened herself against him so tenaciously that had Frankie not been leaning back against the wall, she might have pushed him off-balance. With almost a grunt, he closed her in against his open legs. She threaded her fingers into the thick hair she'd tousled earlier. Her breathing was all shaky; his wasn't any calmer. They kissed with a dizzying side-to-side motion, fevered and seeking, drugging each other with their mouths. Any thought to restricting him in any way abandoned, Kelsey gave herself over to his keeping.

Just the feel of her in his arms drove the breath out of Frankie's lungs. He couldn't touch her enough, hold her enough, kiss her enough. He caressingly explored her through her clothing, his hands gently contouring her breasts, curving her hips, lightly running along her thighs, holding himself back, afraid of moving too quickly. Kelsey made a line of warm kisses around his neck. She pressed her hips closer into his, rejoicing in the sense of wonder at his arousal for her. He found the zipper at the back of her dress and lowered it. His hands were unsteady. His mind was scrambling to understand if she wanted more....

They looked into each other's eyes. There wasn't any question then about what it was they both wanted. He took her hands down from his neck so that he could move her dress off her shoulders. As the loose, gauzy dress came down over her full slip, Kelsey went to step out of it. She didn't have to. Frankie scooped her up into his arms and carried her to the bedroom, leaving the dress behind.

Frankie hit the light switch with his elbow before he placed Kelsey on the bed. He needed to see her—not just her body, but her face and her eyes. "Your eyes drive me crazy," he murmured to her as he lay down at her side. "I need you, Kelsey. I've been going out of my mind wanting you."

"Frankie," Kelsey moaned, and the sound of his name on her lips was the sweetest sound he'd ever heard.

He kissed her cheek and her nose. He touched her one earring. She smiled to him at the gesture and he smiled back. His kiss fell on her shoulder and then on her breast still covered by her full slip and bra. Deep in her body, pulsating throbs exploded with increasing force, bringing an even throatier moan to Kelsey's mouth.

Frankie ripped Kelsey's slip trying to get if off her. "I can't believe how uncoordinated I am with you! I'm actually fumbling."

Kelsey nearly strangled in delight. He was uncoordinated with her.... Just with her.

She helped Frankie get what was left of her slip off. Then she got up on her knees, giving him a full view of her pretty, lace-trimmed beige panties and matching bra. She moved her hands toward the buttons of his shirt, but he blocked the way. Grasping her hips, Frankie placed his mouth to the bare skin between her bra and panties. Kelsey dug her fingers into Frankie's shoulders and her body quivered uncontrollably.

He worked at the clasp of her bra. It took him more time to accomplish the task than it had with any other woman before.

"I'm small," Kelsey said self-consciously, very vulnerable to his first look at her.

He was totally upset by her insecurity. "You're perfect." He wanted her to smile.

Kelsey shook her head, arguing with him.

"You're wrong." His lips nibbled on one bud and then the other. He watched as they hardened for him. "I don't want any of your back talk."

All talk vanished as once again passion and desire took over.

Frankie brought Kelsey down on her back. He placed himself between her thighs while his mouth and tongue teased and tasted. Kelsey made faint, breathy whimpering sounds that excited Frankie beyond reason. He was wild for her.

His lips skimmed over her firm stomach to the line of her panties. Kelsey's back arched and she cried out to him. Hoisting himself up, Frankie slipped her panties part of the way down. Awed, he stared at her. Never had a woman's body thrilled him as much as the sight of Kelsey.

She moaned urgently to him. "Please, Frankie, together..." Her fingers sought for his firmness against his slacks. He lurched and gulped for air.

"I'll be right back," he breathed raggedly to her.

Kelsey hugged herself while Frankie was gone. She was trembling as she'd never trembled before, overwhelmed with the magic he'd created in her. She'd never felt like this. This was the difference between love and attraction.

Frankie came back minus his shirt, loafers and socks, Kelsey saw the small thin foil packet in his hand. She saw something more. She saw indecision flicker in his eyes, but it was gone before she could even think to wonder about it.

Frankie opened his belt buckle and unzipped his fly. He took his slacks and boxer short off all in the same motion. He put the condom on.

He was beautiful, Kelsey's mind registered as she sprawled waiting for him on the bed. Her panties were still around her thighs. Frankie took them down the rest of the way.

Kelsey wrapped her legs tightly around Frankie's hips, clinging to him as he entered her. Their mouths met. Their bodies rocked, caught on fire. There wasn't a chance of waiting for either of them. The wait had already been going on for weeks. Kelsey screamed and buried her mouth against Frankie's neck as she climaxed. Frankie shuddered and ground out her name, falling against her.

For long seconds neither moved as they recouped. Still firm and inside her, Frankie rolled onto his back, taking Kelsey with him. Kelsey knew almost as much pleasure in the way he held her now as she had during their lovemaking. She regarded his face as she traced the outline of his jaw with her finger. He seemed about to say something, but he stopped himself, brought her head to his shoulder and hugged her.

When he could no longer fill her, Frankie turned Kelsey to the bed and left the room. Exhausted and replete, Kelsey dreamily closed her eyes.

Frankie found her asleep when he returned. He smiled at the sight that greeted him. She was curled up into a ball except that one foot dangled over the edge of the bed. He studied the contours of her shoulders, back, buttocks and the one knee drawn up. Carefully he tugged the cover out from under her. Fitting himself next to her, he pulled the cover up over both of them.

He listened to the steady cadence of her breathing, and thought how good it was going to be to wake up with her in the morning.

Chapter Nine

Frankie looked over at Kelsey. She was still asleep. He raised his arm and checked his watch. It was nearly seven o'clock in the morning. Trying not to wake her, Frankie got out of the bed.

Eyes closed, Kelsey counted out fifty to herself. She'd been waiting a half hour now for him to get up and leave so that she could get out of bed. It was difficult enough for her to think of facing him—doing so without her clothes on was more than she could handle. All she could think of now was his girlfriend, Monica. About the only saving grace Kelsey could come up with for herself, on this the morning after, was that she hadn't told him with words how she felt.

Kelsey had no sooner turned the blanket over on her side than she heard Frankie coming back toward the room. Quickly she covered herself up and shut her eyes. The mattress creaked, dipped and Frankie was back under the blanket. Kelsey didn't need her eyes to tell her that he hadn't put any clothes on in the few minutes that he'd been gone.

Doubling his pillow under his neck, Frankie studied the back of Kelsey's head. Her hair was all curly and tangled. His eyes drifted over the outline of her fabulous legs beneath the cover and he groaned to himself just thinking about the feel of her wrapped around his hips.

He eyed the nightstand at his side of the bed where he'd placed the box of condoms that he'd brought back into the bedroom with him. One time with her had hardly been enough, though the fantasy he was having was a real stretch of any male's imagination.

Redefining his physical goals, Frankie closed his eyes. He replayed every second of making love with her, including the one wild moment he'd considered not putting a condom on. Now that he was thinking about that, he couldn't stop thinking about it. Had he wanted to try to make her pregnant?

Kelsey knew Frankie was sleeping again when she heard him snore lightly. Stealthily she slipped her feet to the floor and stood. With one arm in front of her breasts and her other hand place strategically to shield her privacy, Kelsey sidestepped her way alongside the bed. On tiptoe, she made a dash for her robe in the closet. When she had it on, she gingerly opened the bureau drawers for panties, bra, shorts and a shirt. Booty in hand, Kelsey quickly left the bedroom for the bathroom.

Frankie woke for the second time to the sound of the shower running. He hadn't thought about it before, but getting reacquainted in the shower was a dynamite idea. He negated his next thought, which was to intrude on her shower, but he had to shower. He'd invite her to his.

Whistling, Frankie exited the bedroom and went to the hall closet. The dress she'd worn the night before was still on the floor. He carefully hung it up with his clothes.

He wasn't self-conscious about his nudity, but he didn't want to be obvious. After a downward check, Frankie took off the navy shorts he'd just put on and switched to shorts with a fuller cut.

He'd shave first, Frankie decided after running a hand across his jaw. Not for anything in the world would he chance irritating an inch of her gorgeous body.

From his position on the living-room couch Frankie kept an eye on the bathroom door. He didn't have long to wait.

Kelsey came out in a matter of moments. His gaze traveled over her. Her eyes widened on him. He could tell she was surprised at having come upon him as she opened the door. Her hair was still damp, as she hadn't run her blow dryer for long. She'd also gotten fully dressed in green shorts and a matching shirt.

Frankie used the few seconds it took for Kelsey to regain her equilibrium to enjoy the vapor she'd brought into the room from her shower. She smelled of lilacs and rainy days. The lilac scent came from her soap. He knew, because he'd used her soap a couple of times before going to sleep alone in the living room.

He'd caught her off guard. She had rehearsed a small speech during her sojourn in the bathroom. She just couldn't remember a single phrase. What should I say? Kelsey cogitated wildly.

He smiled at her and had to literally force himself not to pounce. "Good morning, beautiful." He got the words out slowly. It was hard for him to speak through the mix of anticipation, impatience and emotion filling his throat.

"Good morning," Kelsey responded stiltedly, and with a strident march she walked by him. She knew what the "beautiful" was all about. It was male talk for "I want more."

What the hell was this? Frankie asked himself, bounding off the couch to follow her to the kitchen.

"Is something wrong?" Frankie inquired, striving for some nonchalance. He didn't need to be hit over the head to catch on that all was not well, though he did speculate that she could be interested in accommodating him if she'd had something heavy in her hand.

Kelsey tilted her chin. "I want it understood that we are not going to even bring up what happened last night." On the spot, Kelsey concluded that the less said was the best way to approach this current situation.

"Why is that?" Frankie braced back against the doorway.

The jerk, Kelsey thought. Couldn't he figure it out? She had half a mind to give his girlfriend a call. She certainly would be doing her a favor.

"Do I have to say it?" Kelsey stared at him.

Frankie made a clicking sound with his tongue. "If you want me to get it, you do."

"Monica," Kelsey elaborated with a flamboyant gesture.

"Oh." Frankie grinned.

Kelsey was astounded at his smile. "Oh... Is that all you have to say?" She couldn't decide whether to beat him with her fists or curse him out.

"I think this is going to give you a laugh—"

"A laugh?" Kelsey flared, adding jujitsu to her list of options.

"If you let me finish speaking you might see the humor in this." Maybe humor wasn't quite the right word. "We broke up. By the way, how do you know her name?"

"Suzie and Esther mentioned her to me." Kelsey's anger yielded slightly to confusion. "What do you mean, you broke up?"

He wanted to ask exactly what she'd been told. "I mean just what I said. We broke up."

Kelsey eyed Frankie with uncertainty. "When?"

"This is the funny part." He tried another smile. "Before we got married."

"You broke up with Monica before we got married," Kelsey reiterated, totally flabbergasted.

"Well, it wasn't so much that I broke up with her. It was a mutual decision."

A stunned expression came over her face. "I asked you about her right after we got married. You said she was okay about all this."

"She obviously was okay about it," he returned.

Kelsey's eyes flashed. "Why didn't you tell me that it was over?"

The glare she was giving him made Frankie think that he stood a better chance against a swarm of bees on the warpath than he did against her at the moment. Regardless, he plunged ahead. "Do you want the truth?"

"Are you sure that wouldn't be too difficult for you?" Kelsey muttered.

"I think I can swing it." He started to formulate an answer in his head first, but she didn't give him much time.

"What is the truth?" Kelsey asked.

"The truth is I had the feeling that you would be calmer about our arrangement if you thought I was involved with someone else. I didn't want you to be nervous that I was free to make a play for you."

Kelsey's mouth dropped open. "When were you going to tell me that you were free?"

"I don't know. I wasn't thinking about it." It had been a long time since he'd given his omission any consideration. He'd forgotten about it.

"I think I know." It was instantly perfectly clear to Kelsey. "You would never have told me if you thought you could get me back in bed without my knowing."

"If that's supposed to make sense to me, it doesn't."

Kelsey did him the honor of explaining. "You wanted sex without commitment. Monica is your built-in out in case things get too sticky for you."

"I have not been thinking of Monica as a built-in out. What's the commitment bit?" The irony did catch up with him. She was already wearing his wedding band on her finger.

"There isn't any commitment bit." Kelsey spoke again before Frankie had the chance to put together another thought. "I'm not interested in any commitment from you. It wasn't you that got me sexually aroused last night. It was just...just one of those... things.''

Frankie winced. "One of those things. Things!"

"Yes." Kelsey turned her back to him, ending her summation. She was not going to have him see tears in her eyes. It was worse knowing that he was free. He could have fallen in love with her, but he hadn't.

Frankie stormed out of the kitchen. It was that or kick in the wall.

Radiating annoyance, the contractor, Paulie Vestry, spread out the blueprints. He was short, stocky and humorless—a pit bull of a guy. "Are these your initials?"

Frankie gave the blueprints a brief glance. Of course they were his initials. He'd put them down when he'd approved the blueprints. Under his F.F. there was K.F. Kelsey was as much a part of all this as he was.

"Yes," Frankie said, fuming, only it wasn't Paulie Vestry that he was fuming at.

"You can take my word," Paulie said unpleasantly. "I do know how to read plans. The bar is exactly the square footage indicated and it's being placed in the exact location the blueprints calls for."

"It doesn't look right," Frankie challenged.

"Why don't you stand to the side and just watch for a while? It will look better to you as we get farther along."

It was clear to Frankie that he was being patronized, but he wasn't up to arguing any longer. He wasn't even all that sure he was right and Paulie was wrong. The only thing he was sure of was that he was all done in. It was only eleven o'clock in the morning, but he felt as if this day had already gone on forever. He'd showered and shaved right after his explosion with Kelsey, leaving the apartment without uttering another word to her.

The front door opened. Frankie was about to yell out that they were closed, which shouldn't have been necessary since there was a sign in the window, when he saw that it was Teddy.

"Hey," Frankie said, crossing the rubble to approach his brother.

Teddy gave Frankie a light playful jab on the shoulder. "Kelsey said I'd probably find you here."

"You spoke to Kelsey?" Frankie asked, tensing.

"Quinn called Kelsey. She and Angie are taking her out for lunch."

"Kelsey accepted?"

"Sure." Teddy eyed Frankie appraisingly. "What's with you?"

"Nothing's with me," Frankie replied sharply.

"Isn't the work going all right?"

"It's going fine."

"So, is there a cold beer around here?"

"Back in the kitchen." Frankie led the way.

Teddy sat at one of the tables that had been moved from up front. Frankie brought over a six-pack from one of the two commercial-size refrigerators.

Teddy popped the cap off one of the bottles. Frankie turned a chair and sat down straddling it. He took a bottle for himself and thumbed off the cap.

"Let me guess," Teddy said smugly. "You and Kelsey had a fight."

Frankie jeered. "I can count off the days we haven't gotten into a fight easier than the days we have."

Teddy rotated his bottle of beer between his hands. "What are the two of you fighting about?"

"Everything," Frankie answered testily.

"Quinn and I used to fight all the time . . . the first time around, anyway."

"Kelsey and I are nothing like you and Quinn." Frankie brought his bottle of beer up to his mouth— great on an empty stomach.

"What makes you say that?" Teddy put his bottle down on the table.

"We're not in love with each other. Is that different enough?"

Teddy leaned back into his seat. "When did the two of you decide you were out of love?"

"Who said we were ever in love?"

Teddy rubbed his face before he fixed his gaze on Frankie again. "Are you telling me that you weren't in love with her when the two of you got married?"

"She wasn't in love with me, either." Frankie drummed his fingers on the table.

"I don't get it." Teddy was confounded. "Why did the two of you get married?"

"She married me to get a green card. I married her for the money to buy Billy DeSilva out and redo the place."

"She paid you to marry her?"

Frankie shook his head. "It was her grandfather...you know Charlie... Charlie had some money put away. He came up with the idea. He wanted her to stay here. She needed to deal with immigration. I needed money."

Teddy inhaled deeply and let it out slowly. "I can't believe you did something like this. I figured you'd gone to the bank."

"Cosmo told me not to waste my time. He told me that no matter how much he shuffled the figures he wasn't going to come up with a profit-and-loss statement a bank would pay out on."

"Why didn't you come to me? I could have co-signed a note for you."

"I didn't want to come to you," Frankie snapped. "Drop it. Okay?"

Teddy dropped that part of it but continued to pursue the other topic. "When I saw the two of you at the party you looked like you could barely keep your hands off her."

"That's got nothing do with anything, even if I haven't kept my hands off her."

"Are you saying that the two of you are sleeping together?"

"Just once," Frankie answered abrasively.

Teddy scratched his head. "When exactly did the one time happen?"

"Last night. Would you like to hear what she had to say about it this morning? She said it was just one of those things . . . a thing! She got aroused, but it had nothing to do with me in particular."

"Ouch. . . . I'm sorry, bro."

Frankie scoffed. "You don't really think I care? Believe me, I can easily survive without touching her again."

"I'm so glad we got together today." Quinn smiled across the table at Kelsey.

"We would have asked you out to lunch sooner if you hadn't been so involved with the renovations at the bar," Angie said. "Nancy was going to join us, but something came up and Lisa is working. We'll do it again on a Saturday when we can all get together, or we can have a ladies' night out."

Kelsey nodded and set a smile on her face. Her first inclination had been to beg out of this invitation to lunch. She hadn't because she couldn't stand the thought of spending the day with herself. Only, she wasn't able to enjoy Angie and Quinn's company. They were real, and warm, and charming. Kelsey Falco was a fake.

Their meals arrived at the table. The restaurant was a small bistro in Greenwich Village and they were seated in the outdoor patio, which looked onto the street. It was a beautiful sunny day. Angie and Quinn wore sleeveless, scooped-neck maternity dresses. Kelsey had on a long cotton skirt with sandals and a short-sleeved blouse.

Angie and Quinn dug in to their cold pasta heaped with avocado, asparagus, shrimp and lobster. Kelsey had followed suit and ordered identically.

Angie looked up from her plate at Kelsey. "We may both be eating for two, but you don't seem to even be eating for one."

"I'm not as hungry as I thought I was," Kelsey answered.

"You haven't been feeling queasy in the morning, have you?" Quinn questioned, and smiled over to Angie.

"No." Kelsey quickly shook her head. "I'm not pregnant. Just a little tired today."

"I bet my brother is keeping you up half the night," Angie teased.

Kelsey's cheeks turned pink. "We...ah...had a fight this morning." She felt she had to explain her despondency.

Quinn smiled. "Don't worry. I'm sure you'll make up tonight."

Angie put in a suggestion. "After we finish lunch we can go shopping for lingerie. Black and scanty always works."

Kelsey's heart dropped hopelessly to the pit of her stomach. "I can't stand lying about all this anymore...." Her agitated voice faded out.

Quinn put down her fork. "Lying about what?"

"What is it, Kelsey?" Angie pressed.

Fighting not to give in to tears, Kelsey sniffled and went for a tissue in her shoulder bag. "We're married, but we're...we're not really married."

"I don't understand," Quinn got in before Angie had the chance.

Kelsey blew her nose. "Frankie and I have an arrangement. I didn't meet him eight months ago. We didn't correspond like we said we had. We knew each other just a few days when we went to Las Vegas and got married."

"Why would the two of you do such a thing?" Angie asked, amazed.

"I need a green card and I can't get one without being married to an American citizen. It didn't seem like a bad idea at the time, but now we're not getting along."

"Frankie agreed to marry you just to help you out?" Quinn questioned delicately. She was still trying to figure out the initial point of Kelsey's revelation.

"Frankie is very fond of my grandfather." Kelsey made a conscious decision not to bring up Frankie's reason for marrying her. She knew that he didn't want anyone in the family to know that he'd needed money and how badly he wanted to prove himself.

Angie thoughtfully chewed a piece of lobster. Swallowing, she said, "Doing something way-out is right up Frankie's alley, but this sounds too way-out even for him. Are you sure there wasn't another reason that he married you other than just being fond of your grandfather?"

"Maybe he fell in love with you, but he just couldn't say it," Quinn proposed. "It happened to me, and it happened to Teddy the first time we saw each other."

"Frankie is not in love with me," Kelsey replied, firmly putting that idea to rest, and then had to blow her nose again.

Quinn reached across the table and gave Kelsey's arm a gentle squeeze. "Have you fallen in love with him?"

"No." Kelsey shook her head violently. That was not something she intended to confess.

Quinn and Angie shared a knowing look.

"We weren't going to say anything to anyone about our arrangement until after it was over...once I got my green card and we got divorced," Kelsey continued, missing the look her sisters-in-law had shared. "I've been feeling awful having you all accept me into the family."

"Why don't we all just think of ourselves as being friends?" Quinn offered. "I don't know about you, but sometimes you meet someone and you feel like you instantly relate. I think we relate.''

"I think so, too," Angie agreed enthusiastically.

Kelsey sniffed. "You're both so terrific."

"Incredible," Sonny said after Angie, Teddy and Quinn had filled him in on what they each knew of Kelsey's and Frankie's situation. They'd just finished having dinner together at Sonny and Angie's place.

"I wonder why Kelsey didn't say anything about the money her grandfather put up?" Teddy asked.

"That's easy," Quinn answered and looked at Angie.

"She didn't want Frankie to look anything less than a saint," Angie filled in.

"Exactly," Quinn corroborated. "She's crazy in love with him."

Angie nodded in agreement.

"I'll tell you what I think," Teddy said. "I think he's crazy in love with her, whether he knows it himself or not."

"Talk about the hand of fate," Sonny said.

Teddy held up his cup of coffee, making a toast. "To the two nitwits. May they figure out their crazy relationship."

The others in the room seconded the sentiment with a wholehearted "To love."

Chapter Ten

It was eight o'clock in the evening when Kelsey returned to the apartment. She'd had dinner with a couple of her soon-to-be colleagues. For the past few days she'd gone to meetings at *Style Magazine,* and had dinner out. The magazine was just a matter of weeks away from starting operations, and she'd taken every opportunity to avoid her "husband."

Surreptitiously Kelsey noted that Frankie was seated in one of the armchairs. The TV was on. The couch was still opened into a bed—he'd stopped bothering to close it before he left the house in the morning. It was almost a month now since the night they'd made love.

Out of the corner of his eye Frankie tracked Kelsey's progress toward the bedroom. He knew the first thing she'd do was change out of the suit she was wearing into something more comfortable. He'd put on shorts and a white T-shirt after he'd gotten back from supervising the renovations at the bar. He expected that she'd had dinner out. He'd had dinner out himself.

As soon as she closed the bedroom door Frankie tried to put his mind on the baseball game. He hadn't been engrossed before she got home. He was even less engrossed now.

Kelsey came out of the bedroom in her green shorts and a beige top, and Frankie gave her a brief glance. She was holding a couple of rolls of film in her hand. She'd begun developing pictures in the bathroom in the evening. The room was large enough, and there was a bridge table in there that she'd borrowed from Charlie. She had asked his permission to turn the bathroom into a darkroom for an hour or so at night. He'd shrugged his okay. That was mostly the way they'd been speaking to each other—gestures or monosyllables. The last full sentences they'd spoken to each other had been in her mother's presence before she'd returned to London. To their advantage, her mother and Charlie had been so preoccupied getting to know each other, neither had noticed the strain.

Not looking over at Frankie, Kelsey walked to the kitchen. She took a bottle of soda out of the refrigerator and poured herself a drink. The Mexican food that she'd tried for the first time was still hot on her tongue.

Kelsey gulped down her glass of soda, her thoughts turning to Frankie. What did he have to be so mad about, anyway? He'd gotten what he'd wanted. He'd gotten sex.

Frankie watched Kelsey start to march by again. He was not looking at her full faced, but he could see her, just the same. She was on the way to the bathroom now with her film. He'd had the pictures that he'd bartered for her jail fine framed today. They were going to be ready in time for the bar's grand reopening.

Kelsey stepped into the bathroom, switching on the light. Three seconds later she came back out, taking a stance at Frankie's side. "What is that hanging in there?"

"Let me guess," Frankie said drolly. "Towels?"

"Not towels," Kelsey replied tautly. "But it is hanging on the towel bar."

Frankie got up off the couch and walked to the bathroom door. Kelsey stepped right behind him.

"Are you referring to my jockstrap?" Frankie inquired indifferently, following the direction of her pointed finger.

"What is it doing hanging there?" Kelsey asked. She was all strung out.

"It's drying," Frankie returned carelessly.

"I can see that," Kelsey rebuked. "Why isn't it downstairs in the laundry room?"

"Because the laundry room is closed now." He shot her the same nasty look she was giving him. "I washed it in the sink. I need it for tomorrow. I'm playing handball."

"I do not want to have to look at your personal body things."

"Am I supposed to be thrilled looking at your bras, panties and panty hose?"

Kelsey righteously crossed her arms in front of her chest. "I happen to have certain bras and panties that have to be washed by hand. They're too delicate for a washing machine and dryer."

"Well, my jockstrap may not be delicate, but it's staying right where it is until it dries."

Kelsey was getting more steamed by the moment. "Do you know what your problem is—"

"Yeah." Frankie sliced into her speech. "You're my problem!"

The phone rang. It rang again.

"Aren't you going to answer it?" Kelsey asked acrimoniously.

"It could just as well be for you. You get calls from Sue and Esther, and my sisters."

"It's your phone." It wasn't just his phone. It was also his towel bar, Kelsey realized, and his bathroom. Damn it!

Pivoting, Frankie headed for the phone in the kitchen.

"I was just about to give up that anyone was home," said the male voice on the other end after Frankie's tight hello.

"We're home," Frankie snapped. The voice wasn't one he recognized. "We're just not buying anything tonight."

"I'm not selling anything. I'm from the immigration department. My name is Timothy Reed."

Frankie's stomach lurched.

"I'd like to come by, if that's all right."

It took Frankie a second to respond. "When did you have in mind?"

"I'm just around the block from you. I decided I'd best stop to call first to be sure you were both at home. My last two surprise visits for today didn't pan out. Neither of those couples were at home."

"Uh-huh," Frankie said, not able to think of anything else to say.

"I'll see you both in a few minutes, then."

"Uh-huh," Frankie said for a second time, uttering an entirely different response under his breath.

The line went dead. Frankie hung up the phone and sprinted back to the bathroom. Kelsey wasn't there. He dashed into the bedroom and found her. She was rummaging in one of the dresser drawers.

"Listen to me calmly," he said as she turned to him. "That was someone from immigration. He's on his way over. He called from around the block. What we've got to do is get the couch in the living room closed and get my clothes from the hall closet into the closet in here. I don't know how thorough the inspection is going to be, but we'd better not take any chances."

Kelsey's knees buckled right before she crumbled onto the side of the bed. "It's over," she said, her eyes appearing to triple in size. "It's all over."

Frankie put his hands under Kelsey's elbows and lifted her to her feet. "It is not over. We have a few minutes. We can do it."

She just shook her head.

Frankie saw Kelsey's bottom lip pucker and his brain clicked. He knew exactly what to do to get her going. Taking her face between his hands, he kissed her harder than he'd ever kissed her before.

"How dare you!" Kelsey was fighting mad when Frankie released her mouth.

Frankie smiled. "Start bringing in my clothes and I'll get the couch."

"Right," Kelsey groaned, and they almost knocked into each other as they both sped out to the living room. Kelsey headed for the hall closet. Frankie went to the opened couch.

"Didn't they say they would notify us when they were planning to come by?" Kelsey called to Frankie as she grabbed a handful of his clothes.

"That's what they said," he answered from the bathroom, dumping his sheets and blanket in the hamper.

They passed each other in the living room. Kelsey was running into the bedroom, her arms loaded down. Frankie ran over to the couch for his pillows and then sprinted into the bedroom. He tossed his pillows into the room. "Put them on top of yours on the bed."

"We're not going to make it," Kelsey moaned, dropping some of Frankie's clothes on the floor as she went to get his pillows.

"Do you want me to take time out to kiss you again?" Frankie asked extemporaneously.

"No," Kelsey answered reactively.

Frankie sent Kelsey a wink, then went back into the living room and finished putting the couch together. He grabbed what was left of his clothes in the hall closet and came into the bedroom. Together they hung up everything on hangers, and brought the clothes that had been on the closet shelf over to the dresser.

Frankie grinned as Kelsey folded one of his shirts. "I don't think neatness is going to count."

Doing as he was doing, Kelsey stuffed the clothes into the drawer.

Perspiration was dripping off both their faces as they finished. Frankie took hold of Kelsey's hand and pulled her to the bathroom. He turned the cold water on, splashed his face, then motioned for her to do the same.

Kelsey soaked her face then reached for a towel, only to wind up with Frankie's jockstrap in her hand. She looked at it expressively.

Frankie hauled Kelsey into his arms. The damp jockstrap was between them as he kissed her again. "I think I may patent this," he teased, tapping his mouth after letting her go.

"I wasn't going to yell about it anymore." Kelsey whacked Frankie's firm abdomen with her fist. It wasn't a hard whack, not that she thought he would have felt it if she'd put her entire weight into it.

"Comb your hair." Frankie smiled. "And put on a dry top."

Kelsey picked up her comb from the shelf where she kept her cosmetics. She ran it through her hair and handed it to him. "You'd better comb yours," she said and left quickly to get a fresh top from the bedroom. She pulled out a shirt for Frankie and threw it to him as she came back out after changing hers.

Clasping his fresh shirt between his thighs, Frankie yanked his wet T-shirt up over his head. "Hamper," he said, flinging it toward Kelsey. Kelsey took it to the bathroom while Frankie changed.

There was a firm rap on the door.

Frankie looked at Kelsey. Her face was still bright from exertion.

Kelsey took a shaky breath. "Should I open it?"

"Sit on the couch. I'll get it." Frankie smiled over at her as he casually opened the front door.

"Timothy Reed," said the balding, middle-aged male, briefcase in one hand, flashing an ID with the other. He looked as if he'd just sucked a lemon.

Frankie pulled in a worried breath at Timothy Reed's less-than-cheerful mood, and introduced himself.

Kelsey got to her feet as soon as Frankie approached the couch with their guest.

"My wife, Kelsey Falco," Frankie introduced.

The immigration agent put out his hand. "Timothy Reed."

Kelsey would have liked to have wiped her palm on her shorts. She knew her hand was sweaty. Going for second best, Kelsey spread her fingers trying to draw some air between each digit before she clasped the man's hand.

"Before we speak," Mr. Reed began, "I'd like to take a look around the apartment, if you don't mind?"

"We don't mind," Frankie answered and slung his arm around Kelsey's waist.

Without further preamble, the older man walked into the bedroom. Kelsey and Frankie stood in place, leaning in unison from side to side trying to keep their eyes on the immigration agent.

Timothy Reed headed straight for the closet. Kelsey and Frankie spared each other a glance when he looked inside. When he closed the closet door, both Kelsey and Frankie sighed under their breath.

The immigration agent stayed in the bedroom a few minutes longer, opening drawers, poking around. He came out, walked into the bathroom and then the kitchen. All in all, he couldn't have roamed any longer than ten minutes before coming back to the living room. For Kelsey and Frankie it was the longest six hundred seconds on record.

"Could I make you a cup of coffee?" Kelsey asked as Mr. Reed sat down in an armchair. She was still standing with Frankie in front of the couch. They were locked together by Frankie's arm.

"A cup of coffee sounds good," the agent responded, and got up from the armchair. "We can all sit in the kitchen."

With Timothy Reed seated at the table, Kelsey set up the coffeemaker. Frankie put water in the teakettle for Kelsey. While the coffeemaker and the teakettle did their thing, Kelsey put mugs on the table and a tea bag for herself.

"I understand that you have a bar and grill," Agent Reed said as Frankie came to the table with the sugar bowl and a pitcher of milk.

"We're in the process of renovating right now. Kelsey did the decorating," Frankie answered, contemplating Kelsey as she stood by the stove with her back to him. For as much as he tried, he couldn't figure out where he stood with her. All he knew for certain was that he had her under his skin and that he missed just talking to her.

The water was starting to roll to a boil. Kelsey turned the burner off before the kettle whistled. She brought it to the table and filled her mug. When she went to check on the coffee, Frankie dunked her tea bag into her cup.

Reed looked on, observing.

Minutes later, sipping his coffee, which he took with three heaping teaspoons of sugar, no milk, Mr. Reed

said, "I read in your application that you have a job
lined up with a magazine." His attention was fixed on
Kelsey.

"Yes." Kelsey nodded. "We've already gotten together for meetings. They've been going very well."
Her last remark was for Frankie. She'd wanted to talk
to him about the magazine and her impressions of the
people she'd be working with. She'd wanted to talk to
him about the renovations. She wanted to talk to him
about her mother and Charlie.

As if he'd just read her mind, Frankie volunteered,
"Kelsey's mother was here for a short visit."

"Her first time to the States?" Reed asked.

"Yes," Kelsey answered. "She came to meet Frankie. She said she suspected when I came back home
after being here eight months ago that something special had happened to me."

"I understand that you corresponded with each
other." Timothy Reed took a file from his briefcase
and opened it on the table.

"Yes." Kelsey answered before Frankie.

"Did Frank propose to you by mail?" The agent
glanced up at Kelsey from his notes.

"No..." Kelsey stumbled. She should have said yes.
Of all the details they'd gone over together, the actual
proposal was something they hadn't covered.

Frankie intervened. "She came back sooner than we
both expected because she'd gotten this great job offer."

Agent Reed swallowed down some coffee, then gave
Kelsey his sharp regard. "Were you aware that your
application for a green card would have been turned
down if it was just for a work permit? We only make

allowances for foreigners to fill jobs here that cannot be readily filled by one of our own citizens."

"We found that out when we went to speak to an immigration attorney," Frankie responded. "I can tell you that I did use that to my advantage. I would have courted Kelsey no matter how long it took, but I did prefer being able to speed her along. All's fair in love."

"Sped her right to Vegas, I see." Agent Reed focused on Frankie.

"I wasn't going to give her a chance to change her mind," Frankie countered easily.

The agent moved on to Kelsey. "You didn't mind not having the usual wedding fuss?"

"I didn't want to give him a chance to change his mind," Kelsey answered pertly, playing her part.

Frankie gave Kelsey a teasingly provocative look. "You could have told me that I didn't have to work myself into a sweat. I'm going to get you back for that later."

She remembered him saying something quite similar when they'd been playing with each other right before they'd made love. She almost lost her place in the sham they were putting on for the agent. Not able to come up with a retort, Kelsey put a seductive smile on her face to equal his.

"Oh, yeah..." Frankie said sexily. Putting his hand out, he captured the back of Kelsey's neck. Leaning, he kissed her lightly.

This time the smile she gave him was warm and genuine. She knew the reason he'd just kissed her was to keep her spirits up. She could see it in his eyes.

Agent Reed coughed. "How did the two of you happen to meet?"

"I came to see my grandfather. He works for my Frankie." Kelsey finger combed her hair from her face. She was suddenly very warm.

"You seem to have lost an earring," the agent commented.

"She only wears one," Frankie said. "It's a theory she's trying out."

"What theory is that?"

Frankie answered. "Some art critic told her that she wasn't putting enough of her heart into her photos. She's got this idea in her head that wearing one earring is going to remind her to be more daring. I don't think that art critic knew what he was talking about."

Kelsey's heart raced, acutely aware that he meant what he was saying.

"Is your theory working?" Reed asked.

"I'm still testing it out," Kelsey answered, slow to take her eyes away from Frankie.

Three-quarters of an hour later Agent Reed put his hand over his empty mug as Kelsey made to refill his cup for the third time. "I don't think I'm going to need anything more." He put the file in his briefcase, snapped it shut, pushed back his seat and stood.

"When will we hear something?" Frankie asked, getting to his feet along with Kelsey.

"Anywhere from a week to ten days. Perhaps a little longer. We're always backed up."

Kelsey and Frankie accompanied the agent to the door. From the hallway he said, "Have a good evening," and left.

Frankie closed the door. Kelsey went to the couch and sank down. Frankie sat next to her.

"I think he went for the full package," Frankie evaluated.

"You were incredible." Kelsey looked into Frankie's face.

"So were you." He gazed back at her.

"You covered up for me." She looked away. "Frankie, I don't want to keep acting the way we've been acting with each other."

"I don't, either," he replied, inhaling quickly.

Kelsey practiced saying in her head, "I love you," and thought of saying it out loud—laying it out there like a big, fat bomb. "The trouble with sex is that it's so sexual, but I guess men don't see it that way."

"There's sex and there's great sex," Frankie said, trying to calculate the best stand to be taking at a moment like this. Part of him believed every word she'd said to him the morning after. Part of him didn't. At the moment that part of his libido was calling the shots.

Kelsey got off the couch and sat on one of the armchairs. "Sometimes the most sensible arrangement doesn't turn out exactly as planned."

Frankie rotated his head from side to side. The muscles in his neck were tight. "We could try going back to square one."

"There's something I need to tell you." Kelsey dropped her eyes to her lap. At least he'd spared her the humiliation of saying he loved her in the throes of passion when it would have just been something men say. "I told Angie and Quinn the truth about our arrangement, but I didn't tell them the part about

Charlie putting up money for you to redo the bar...just that you'd married me to help me get a green card."

"I told Teddy all of it," Frankie revealed. "By now Sonny and Nancy and Shep know...maybe even Lisa."

Kelsey felt a sinking feeling in her stomach. "Will they tell your parents? I really think we should be the ones to tell them."

"They would have been over here, or on the phone by now, if they'd been told. I think we should wait until after we've heard from immigration to tell them. They might still be called for an interview. Why make it hard for them to lie?"

Kelsey nodded and thought about having to tell her mother the truth about her marriage. She didn't want to continue on with this conversation. "My mother is staying in touch with Charlie. They've written to each other twice since she's been home."

"That's good, Kelsey."

"I had this fantasy that the three of us would become as close as your family is with each other." Kelsey chewed her bottom lip. "But it isn't like that."

"Your grandfather and your mother have a lot of making up to do. It's going to take time." He gave her his take on the situation.

"I still feel awkward around Charlie." Kelsey's hand moved up and down the arm of the chair. "I thought I wouldn't, but I do."

"Maybe you need to give yourself permission to feel natural with him."

She stared into space for a moment. "Do you think it would be inappropriate if we invited Angie and

Sonny and Quinn and Teddy over for dinner one night...Nancy and Shep and Lisa, too?" Kelsey allowed herself the feeling that they might really become friends.

"I don't think it would be inappropriate," Frankie answered carefully. "We could prepare it together."

Kelsey looked for something more to say. "I wonder if there's anything good on the telly tonight?"

"I could turn it on and we can flick through the channels." He didn't know what he would do if she got up to go into the bedroom to watch it in there.

"All right." Kelsey turned to better face the TV. It would be okay just as long as they didn't watch anything romantic. She couldn't handle anything romantic right now.

Letting out the breath he'd been holding, Frankie reached for the remote control.

Chapter Eleven

Kelsey came back into the kitchen after changing clothes for their company's arrival. She had on a jersey turquoise tank dress with buttons down the front and a flared skirt. Kelsey saw that Frankie had put on black slacks and a gray shirt in the bathroom while she'd been in the bedroom.

"I think we've got this recipe down to a science," Frankie told her as he gave the sour cream sauce on top of the stove an unnecessary stirring. His eyes were on her face, though he was well aware of the fit of her dress over her hips and that the cut of the neckline showed off her creamy skin.

"I hope it all tastes as good this time as when we made it for my mother and grandfather." She expected any day now to find out if she was going to get a green card. Whichever way it went, she'd be moving out. Heavyhearted, Kelsey gazed over at him.

Stop looking at her, Frankie said to himself, and answered, "It will." His eyes stayed put with a force of their own.

Her knees suddenly weak, Kelsey sat at the table. "It's too bad Lisa can't make it tonight." She crossed her legs, deliberately fixing her dress to show them off. Idiotically, she'd given herself the idea that if they became lovers he might fall in love with her. Only he hadn't made any move in that direction and she wasn't brazen enough to be any more overt than she was being.

"Great dress, by the way." He dragged his eyes from her legs back to her face.

"Thank you," Kelsey answered politely. "It's cool and comfortable. I just bought it." She hadn't bought it because it was cool or comfortable. She'd bought it because she thought it looked good on her.

Pushing back against the counter, Frankie glanced at his watch as a diversion. His nerves were rubbed raw. "They should be here pretty soon." There had been moments in the week since Agent Reed's visit that he'd been certain she wanted him to make a sexual advance toward her. What he couldn't figure out was why he wasn't going for it. He had needs. She had needs.

"I'm glad they all know about our arrangement." Fruitless as it was, Kelsey dipped her shoulders in a way she thought might be alluring. "We won't have to pretend for them."

"Yeah." He didn't have anything else to say on the subject. He had all he could do to keep his mind on any subject but one. Did she know she was enticing him right now?

Kelsey felt pins and needles begin in one leg from sitting so stiffly posed. She got up and walked into the living room.

She'd taken the bridge table out of the bathroom and they'd bought two others, as well as several folding chairs. She'd already pushed the tables together, covered them with a cloth and set the dishes, glasses and silverware out.

Frankie watched her move around the makeshift table. Getting the bar reopened was the only thing he should have on his mind. It was the only thing he had any control over. He certainly didn't have any control over his relationship with her—whatever that was.

The doorbell rang, and they both jumped.

"I'll get it," Kelsey called out and a second later opened the door.

Angie, Sonny, Nancy and Shep had come together. They didn't live far from one another.

"I'll take the booze," Frankie said, coming up alongside Kelsey.

Sonny and Shep gave Frankie the bottles they were holding. Sonny shadowboxed Frankie a punch after they'd all come in.

Nancy and Angie both handed Kelsey cake boxes. "They both have to go in the refrigerator," Angie said.

The three women walked to the kitchen while the men stayed in the living room.

"You look wonderful," Nancy told Kelsey.

Kelsey smiled. "So do both of you."

"I look like a blimp," Angie moaned. "I hate the two of you."

Nancy laughed. "You are not that big."

The doorbell rang again, and Kelsey saw Frankie go and get it. Moments later Quinn was in the kitchen and Teddy was hanging out with the men. Quinn put a cellophane-covered tray of nuts, imported chocolate and dried fruit on the kitchen table.

"Are you sure you're pregnant?" Angie comically grumbled to Quinn.

"I'm showing." Quinn flattened her generously cut beige dress over her rounding stomach.

"Right." Angie made a face. "Give me a break."

"You're two and a half months in front of me." Quinn grinned.

Would she ever know what it was like to be pregnant? Kelsey wondered, making room in the refrigerator for the cakes that Nancy and Angie had brought. Would she ever be even married for real? She wanted to have Frankie's babies....

"What would the two of you like to drink?" Frankie addressed Angie and Quinn as he entered the kitchen.

"Ginger ale, if you have it," Quinn answered.

"We've got it." Frankie went to Kelsey's side at the refrigerator. Kelsey took out the platter of tea sandwiches she'd made to serve as an appetizer.

"Have you got something diet?" Angie questioned.

"What kind do you want?" Frankie asked. "I'll run out."

"I don't want you to run out on my account. I'll have some water with ice."

Frankie grinned over at Angie. "Hey, moppet, you know I'd do it for you. Just say the word."

"Don't call me moppet!" Angie made a face at Frankie. "Sonny, my brother is bothering me."

Sonny called back from the living room, "Leave your sister alone and bother your wife."

Kelsey and Frankie avoided meeting each other's eyes.

"Did you make those?" Nancy asked, looking at the tray of tea sandwiches Kelsey was holding.

Kelsey nodded and extended the tray to Nancy, then Quinn, then Angie. They each took one.

"Don't we get any service out here?" Teddy called into the kitchen.

Kelsey walked into the living room with the platter. Quinn, Angie and Nancy came along with her. They sat on the couch while Kelsey extended the tray to Teddy, Sonny and Shep. They were sitting on chairs they'd turned around from the table.

"This is great," Sonny said after taking a bite. "What am I eating?"

Kelsey looked at the side of Sonny's sandwich after she'd placed the platter down on the coffee table. "I think that one is cream cheese and anchovies."

"Nance, you going to have wine?" Frankie asked, handing Quinn a large glass of ginger ale and Angie a large glass of water with ice.

"Red." Nancy nodded.

"White wine, Kelsey?" Frankie asked. Their eyes met.

"Yes, thank you." Kelsey diverted her gaze.

Frankie turned to the men as Kelsey sat in one of the armchairs. "Name your poison, guys."

The three men asked for Scotch on the rocks. Frankie made the same for himself. He handed everyone his drink.

Teddy looked over at his brother, and then at Kelsey. "I'm sure the two of you are wondering if we're going to bring up your situation, so to cut to the chase, we are. How are the two of you doing?"

Frankie glanced at Kelsey. "Hey, we're doing... We're doing just fine."

"Fine." Kelsey duplicated Frankie's response.

"So, where are things at?" Sonny inquired, taking another tea sandwich.

"We had a visit from immigration," Kelsey answered.

"How did that go?" Nancy asked.

"We think it went okay," Kelsey replied, remembering how they'd rushed around. Remembering how he'd kissed her. Remembering that was when they'd begun this tense truce.

"How's that new group you're working on?" Frankie asked Teddy, changing the subject.

"Good." Teddy nodded. "Listen, when the two of you are ready to get divorced, let me know. I'll speak to Quinn's father. He can pull some strings and get it through for you quick."

Kelsey's heart jumped and stayed suspended.

Frankie sent Teddy a riled look. "Thanks, but no thanks. We got ourselves into this, we can get ourselves out of it when we're ready."

"You don't have to jump down my throat," Teddy sparred back, but the corners of his mouth were raised amusedly.

"I'm not jumping down your throat." Frankie tried to get back his cool.

"Sounds like you are," Sonny put in.

Kelsey got to her feet. Frankie's eyes went immediately over to her. "I think that chicken is going to get overcooked if we don't take it out now."

"Yeah, we'd better get the chicken out," Frankie agreed.

While Kelsey and Frankie went to the kitchen, their guests passed each other satisfied looks.

"There's Angie standing there trying to figure out what to do," Sonny continued. "Keep in mind, I'm not budging. I want to meet this guy that Nancy's supposedly set her up with.... I'll take another slice of that chocolate cake, Kelsey."

Kelsey cut Sonny another slice. "What happened next?"

"I finally tell Sonny that my date isn't coming to pick me up. I'm going to meet him at the movie theater." Angie took up the story. "Now, I've already told Sonny that I'm going to be bringing Melissa and Lindsay to Nancy's house for them to sleep over. Only, I'm so flustered at this point that I walk out and forget about taking the girls with me."

Sonny took the story back. "I go to the phone and call Nancy to tell her that Angie isn't going to be bringing the girls over, that I'm going to stay and baby-sit."

"I don't know that Angie has made up this story for Sonny." Nancy filled in her part. "When Sonny calls I let out of the bag that I never fixed Angie up with a blind date."

Kelsey smiled over to Angie. "Why did you lie to Sonny about having a blind date to begin with?"

"I was trying to head him off, because I knew I was in love with him." Angie grinned.

Kelsey's bright eyes were dancing. "But wait a minute. Were any of you married by an Elvis Presley impersonator?"

Frankie winked at Kelsey. "We've topped them there."

"An Elvis Presley impersonator." Teddy laughed. "You're joking?"

Kelsey shook her head. "His sideburns were fake. At least, I thought they were." Kelsey looked to Frankie.

Frankie smiled. "Fake."

"He was not happy with us," Kelsey said, smiling back at Frankie.

"How come?" Teddy asked.

The doorbell rang.

Frankie got up. "Maybe Lisa decided to make it, after all."

Everyone looked to the hallway while Frankie opened the door.

"Does Kelsey Shepherd live here?" asked the male standing at the threshold.

Deep down in his gut Frankie knew instantly who he was facing. "Kelsey Falco," Frankie rectified at a quick clip.

Eric Montgomery looked confused. Frankie looked him over. He was technically handsome, conservative and clean-cut.

Hearing her name, Kelsey left the table and came to the door. Her eyes widened. "Eric..." Kelsey was shocked. "How did you know where to find me?"

"I called the magazine. They gave me this address. I was going to call here first, but then I decided to surprise you."

Frankie sucked air through his teeth. "Why don't you come in?" He couldn't come up with any other choice, except to let Kelsey stand at the door talking to him.

In something of a daze, Kelsey stepped with Frankie to the side to make room for Eric to enter.

All eyes from the table were fixed on the hallway.

Eric took in the rest of the clan before his eyes came back to Kelsey. "I can see this is a bad time. Why don't I just call you?"

Kelsey would have much preferred that. This moment was embarrassing for her.

"It's no problem. We're just having coffee." Frankie preferred now to setting up the privacy of a phone call.

Eric extended his hand to Frankie. "Eric Montgomery."

"Frankie Falco." Frankie allowed himself the luxury of being aggravated.

The handshake was brief but firm on both sides. Two male energies crossing swords.

Frankie walked to the table with Kelsey and Eric behind him.

"Falco?" Eric questioned in an aside to Kelsey.

Frankie had no problem hearing Eric's question. He assumed Kelsey nodded her head. She hadn't said anything. Had she given Eric a silent message with her expressive eyes?

Frankie took care of the introductions. "Sit down." Frankie motioned Eric to his seat. "Eric is an old friend of Kelsey's."

"Where do you and Kelsey know each other from?" Teddy asked as Eric sat down.

"I met Kelsey when I was in London on business."

Kelsey followed Frankie into the kitchen. He was going for another chair. She was going for another place setting. They didn't look at each other.

"What business are you in, Eric?" Sonny was asking when Frankie and Kelsey returned.

"Advertising. I'm an account exec with Schuster, Schuster and Lyman. I buy TV time."

Frankie fit his chair in at the table opposite Eric... and Kelsey.

Kelsey put the place setting down in front of Eric. Frankie took note of the small, unreadable look they exchanged before Kelsey reached for the thermos server filled with coffee. She poured Eric a cup, then got the pitcher of milk and the bowl of sugar, and placed them convenient to his reach.

"Can I slice you a piece of cake?" Kelsey asked, still standing. Her shock at finding Eric at the front door had worn off. Now she was just angry at Frankie for making this harder on her by insisting that Eric join them.

"No, thank you." Eric shook his head.

Kelsey sat down.

Conspicuous quiet followed and gathered momentum.

Nancy broke into it. "Are you married, Eric?"

"Separated," Eric replied. "Officially separated. We're talking with our attorneys right now regarding the settlement of our marital estate."

Frankie's eyes shot to Kelsey. He couldn't tell what her reaction was to Eric's news bulletin. She wasn't giving anything away. Neither was she meeting his look.

"Do you have children?" Angie asked.

"We have a five-year-old daughter. We're seeing a family therapist to make certain we handle the situation as best as possible for our daughter's sake."

Frankie did see a reaction on Kelsey's face this time. He would have bet anything that she hadn't known he had a child. "Would anyone like an after-dinner drink?"

"I'll take a brandy," Teddy answered.

"That sounds good," Shep agreed.

Sonny assented, and so did Eric.

Kelsey stood. "I'll get the glasses." She hadn't known that Eric had a daughter. Another detail he'd neglected to mention back in London. He hadn't even mentioned it when she'd shown up in New York.

Nancy had a small taste of Irish Cream liqueur. Kelsey joined her. Angie and Quinn each had a little more decaffeinated coffee.

"I didn't think you knew anyone in New York except for your mother's father," Eric commented to Kelsey, brandy in hand.

"My grandfather works for Frankie," Kelsey answered succinctly.

"How long have the two of you been married?" Eric used a tone of voice used for small talk.

"We got married so that I could get my green card."
Kelsey was not in the mood to play games. She certainly did not have to lie for anyone at the table.

"I see." Eric polished off his brandy and regarded
Frankie. "What business are you in?"

"I own a bar and grill." Frankie felt as if a tourni-
quet had circled his gut and was being turned tighter
and tighter.

"It's going to be a jazz club now," Angie put in.
"Kelsey and my brother have renovated the place.
Kelsey did the decorating. Right, Kelsey?"

"Your brother came up with as many ideas as I
did." Please, Kelsey prayed, let this evening end.

"I think we should be going," Sonny said to Angie.

Since Angie and Sonny had come in Shep's car,
Nancy and Shep got up, as well.

Kelsey and Frankie saw the four of them to the
door.

Quinn and Teddy had begun carrying the mugs,
glasses, silverware and plates into the kitchen when
Kelsey and Frankie returned to the table.

"I'll take over," Kelsey said.

Quinn insisted on helping. Teddy sat down again
with Frankie and Eric.

"How's the advertising game?" Teddy asked.

"We're pretty busy," Eric answered.

Frankie watched Eric take note of Kelsey's move-
ments in the kitchen.

Finally Quinn and Kelsey returned, the dishes ac-
counted for and in the dishwasher.

"I guess we should be going," Quinn said to Teddy.

"If you need a lift, we could give you one," Teddy said to Eric.

"I appreciate the offer, but I have my own car."

Teddy rose, but Eric remained seated. When Kelsey and Frankie made to walk Quinn and Teddy to the door, Teddy said, "That's okay. We can see ourselves out."

Quinn gave Kelsey a hug. Teddy affectionately ruffled Kelsey's hair.

And then there were three....

If Frankie hadn't considered that he would be making fool of himself by literally tossing Eric out the door, he would have. Who really was the odd man out in this scenario?

"Could we go for a ride?" Eric asked Kelsey. "I would like to speak to you."

What was left of Frankie's gut reverberated.

"All right," Kelsey replied quietly. What she had to say to Eric she wanted said now. She did not want to dwell on it. "I won't be long." Kelsey sent Frankie a brief glance.

And then there was one....

Frankie played every psychological trick he could think to play on himself while Kelsey was gone. He didn't get anywhere except to empty half a bottle of brandy down his throat. He was well on his way to being officially soused when Kelsey returned an hour later.

Frankie jerked his head her way as she came up to him. He was still seated at the table.

"I told him that whatever there had been between us is over," Kelsey said simply, her heart on her sleeve.

"You don't owe me a recap," Frankie responded abruptly.

"I didn't say that I did." Turning on her heels, Kelsey walked to the bedroom and closed the door.

At the table Frankie dropped his head to his hands.

Chapter Twelve

Kelsey wiped the steam from her shower off the bathroom mirror. She started towel-drying her hair then stopped as her gaze settled on a bottle of Frankie's after-shave lotion. She looked at his blue toothbrush next to her yellow one, the toothpaste they shared. He always remembered to put the cap on. She didn't. Kelsey put it back on now with tears streaming down her face.

Frankie paced around the living room. He was just about ready. He had on a white jacket and tuxedo slacks that he'd rented for the occasion. All he had left to do was play with the black bow tie hanging undone under the collar of his white dress shirt. It was more than an hour before the bar's grand opening party for his family and friends.

Throat dry, Frankie went into the kitchen and opened the refrigerator for a cold drink, then forgot the drink and took out Kelsey's jar of orange marmalade. It was practically empty. He looked to see if she'd made note on the shopping list hanging by a magnet to the outside of the refrigerator door. She hadn't. He banged the refrigerator door closed and raked his fingers through his hair. In the past three days, since Eric Montgomery's visit, they hadn't uttered a word to each other that hadn't referenced the bar.

Her hair a mass of blown-dry waves and curls, Kelsey applied her makeup paying special attention to her puffy eyes. How could she have expected him to fall in love with her? She was difficult and too structured, and he was loose and daring. She didn't have a great figure, and she couldn't even cook. What could she expect him to see in her?

"I'm going down to see if there's any mail," Frankie called out at the next pass he made in front of the closed bathroom door. He couldn't pace the room anymore.

Kelsey heard the front door close. She opened the bathroom door. Having done all she could with her face, Kelsey headed for the bedroom to change out of her robe and into another new dress. She didn't know why she'd splurged. There wasn't a single point to being even the slightest bit hopeful.

Frankie stood at the mailbox and stared at the envelope addressed to Kelsey from the Department of Immigration. Sure, he wanted the news to be what she wanted, but either way it spelled the end of their make-believe marriage. Disgusted with himself, Frankie weighed the possibility of not giving her the envelope.

Frankie was sitting on the couch, his frame stretched back against the cushion, when Kelsey stepped out of the bedroom. He thought she looked devastatingly beautiful tonight.

Her dress was rayon challis with a sweetheart neckline, stand-away sleeves, fitted bodice and sweeping, calf-length skirt. Lilac rose print against a white background. Kelsey wore it with white slingback pumps.

Carefully avoiding his eyes, Kelsey asked, "Do you need help with your bow tie?" She thought he looked incredibly handsome.

He'd forgotten about his tie. "There was mail for you." He gestured with his eyes to the coffee table.

Kelsey knew what it was even before she picked up the envelope. Her hand was trembling as she slit open the flap.

Frankie watched Kelsey's expression as she read the enclosure. He thought it was bad news, and he cursed himself for having given it to her tonight. The evening's celebration was as much hers and it was his— even if he hadn't been able to work up any excitement.

"They approved me," Kelsey said quietly.

"They did?" He would have thought she'd be jumping up and down, doing that jig she'd done the night her mother had come for dinner with Charlie.... The night they'd made love....

"Hey, that's great. Really great."

Kelsey nodded, holding the letter in one hand, hugging her waist with the other.

The things they weren't saying to each other seemed to reverberate in the quiet.

Making a grand effort to appear nonchalant, Frankie got up and walked to the bathroom. He attended to his tie in front of the medicine-cabinet mirror. Five minutes later they left for the club. They made the trip without speaking.

Charlie walked up to Kelsey and Frankie as soon as they stepped through the front door. He'd come in earlier with Eddie to direct the caterers in setting up. Eddie was across the way still checking over the buffet. He'd be a guest for the rest of the night, as would everyone else who worked for Frankie.

Charlie smiled at Kelsey. "You look lovely."

"You look very dashing yourself," Kelsey responded, admiring her grandfather in his navy blue suit.

Frankie watched the visual interplay, taking in the warm expression Kelsey now freely allowed. It wasn't going to be too long for them to reach the stage when a hug would come naturally. Frankie listened for Kelsey to say she was getting her green card. But she didn't bring it up.

"The musicians are here," Eddie called out. He sent a wolf whistle over to Kelsey.

Kelsey smiled and waved, then turned back to Charlie. "Is there anything I can do?"

"Everything is under control," Charlie answered. "I'm just going to make sure they've brought enough shrimp."

Damn it, Frankie thought, I should have been the one to tell her how good she looks. "I'd better go see to the musicians," was all he could say now.

Left alone, Kelsey started a tour of the room, trying to see it as others were going to see it for the first time.

The original fixtures, all mood-dimmed, were hanging polished from the cleaned, stamped-metal ceiling. The walls painted a smoky blue were an exact match to the new carpeting. There were still quite a number of tables, though they'd made room for an ample dance floor. The tables were covered with white cloths and each was accommodated by a red suede half-moon sofa booth. Tonight there were fresh flowers on every table—bouquets of red and blue blooms. The ambience was red, hot and blue.

Kelsey stopped short. Frankie had added something since she'd seen the final touches just the day before. On a pillar to one side of the bar just beneath one of the fixtures, this one with a brighter bulb, he'd hung her photographs tastefully framed in brass.

Kelsey felt Frankie come up to her side even before her gaze turned his way. "When did you . . ."

"When I went out this afternoon." Frankie's heart jammed against his chest as he saw her eyes become all sparkly. "Are the frames right?"

Kelsey nodded her head. She was too overcome for words and had to struggle to hold back a fresh wave of tears. He hadn't mentioned her photographs for some time now. She'd assumed he'd forgotten about them.

The band started to play. The blues singer began to sing. Kelsey and Frankie could both hear people coming in.

"If you'll excuse me . . ." She didn't wait for him to respond before rushing off to the ladies' room.

When Kelsey came out after reapplying makeup around her eyes, she was instantly surrounded by Angie, Nancy and Quinn. The three women were beautifully dressed.

"We were just coming in to find you," Quinn said.

"The place looks fantastic." Nancy smiled.

Angie, as ever radiant, echoed Nancy's appraisal.

Lisa came over and singled Quinn out. "Teddy pulled Johnny aside to talk to him. Quinn, please make Teddy stop."

"You know your brother," Quinn responded appeasingly.

"If it isn't Teddy," Lisa said, aggravated, "it's Frankie. When are those two going to let me take care of my own life?"

Quinn smiled. "Probably never." She left with Lisa to try to minimize the man-to-man talk Teddy was intent on having with Johnny.

"Where's Sonny and Shep?" Kelsey asked.

"They're having a drink with Frankie at the bar," Angie answered. "Come on. Let's go join them."

With a sick and empty feeling Kelsey moved with her sisters-in-law to the bar.

Shep smiled over to Kelsey. "You did super, kid."

Sonny added, "I hate to think what Frankie would have come up with on his own."

"I wouldn't have been able to come up with a single thought if Frankie hadn't first decided to turn the place into a jazz club," Kelsey said without looking over at him.

Frankie reached for and quietly handed Kelsey a glass of white wine.

Connie and Anthony Falco came over, all thrilled. Anthony gripped Frankie's hand, then clapped his son on the back. "You've got something here. You've really got something here. A jazz club was a good idea."

"Thanks, Dad." Frankie smiled and his eyes found Kelsey. And Kelsey lost herself for a brief emotional moment to share Frankie's pleasure. This was what he had worked for.

"Didn't I tell you he was going to have something?" Connie poked her husband.

"You told me." Anthony nodded, smiling.

Frankie handed his mother and father each a glass of champagne. Anthony Falco raised his. "Ah, *salute*. To life and to love."

"And more grandchildren," Connie Falco said before anyone got in a sip.

Frankie broke into the toast, knowing it was causing Kelsey discomfort. "Kelsey, we really should mingle."

Putting down her wine, Kelsey took the hand Frankie offered.

They made the rounds of countenances. For the sake of the night, they even managed a subdued version of their husband-and-wife act.

The liquor flowed. The braising trays emptied. Kelsey and Frankie parted from each other, returned to each other, then parted again as they were each drawn into separate circles. Cosmo, the accountant, cornered her. Kelsey saw Frankie at the bar talking to Teddy. "Kelsey, you have to make sure he holds on to all the receipts for whatever he buys, no matter how small they are. I've got a feeling this place is going to be a gold mine. We're going to be digging for write-offs." Peripherally, Kelsey caught sight of Frankie coming toward them.

"You've had her ear long enough," Frankie said when he arrived. "We haven't even danced yet."

Heart tripping, Kelsey found herself in Frankie's arms. "Your cousin Cosmo wants you to be sure to hold on to all receipts."

"Uh-huh," Frankie answered briefly.

Kelsey tried with her hand to Frankie's chest to keep a discreet distance between their bodies, but Frankie wasn't having any of that. He took her restraining hand, brought it up to his neck and eliminated the space between them.

Kelsey stepped on Frankie's toe. "I'm sorry." She was flushed and bothered both physically and emotionally.

"You're all tense," was Frankie's response.

Giving in to his rhythm, Kelsey let her body just move with his. "Aren't you tense?"

"Yes." Tense hardly said it.

"You shouldn't be tense. Your cousin Cosmo said this place is going to be a gold mine. If he's saying it, it's got to be true." She wanted him to know that she felt it, as well.

He wondered just how long he'd been in love with her without consciously realizing it. "Have you told your grandfather about getting your green card?"

"Not yet." With a will of its own, Kelsey's hand now clung even tighter around Frankie's neck.

The music ended and the band picked then to take a break.

"I'm not giving you a divorce," Frankie said matter-of-factly as he stepped back, setting Kelsey from him. If nothing else, he was going to put some time on his side.

"What?" Kelsey blinked.

"You heard me," Frankie replied, and walked away.

Kelsey would have rushed right after him if she hadn't been in shock and he hadn't been immediately swallowed up by a group. When Kelsey finally got moving, Connie Falco intercepted her.

"Kelsey, did you eat something?" Connie asked. "I didn't see you eat anything."

"Yes, I have." Kelsey spotted Frankie walking toward the kitchen. "I'm going to get something more to eat right now."

Frankie was alone in the kitchen when Kelsey marched in.

"I know what you're worried about." Kelsey stood steely in front of him. Her sensible, structured mind had arrived at a conclusion.

"Really?" Frankie cocked his head. "What am I worried about?"

"I am not going to make any financial demands on you no matter how successful this place is." Kelsey set the record straight.

"I thought you had already figured out that I don't have all that much interest in money," Frankie answered lackadaisically.

"Then why aren't you going to give me a divorce?" Kelsey ran her hair off her face in the way she did when she was intent or nervous.

"You're wearing two earrings." He stared at her.

"I know!" Kelsey gave Frankie her sternest look. "You haven't answered me about the divorce."

Frankie grinned at the stormy face she was giving him. Stormy face and all, he loved her. "You tell me why you're wearing two earrings and I'll answer you."

"I asked you first," Kelsey retorted.

"We can stand here all night and have a stalemate." He was teasing her now, because he knew the answer. He didn't know how he knew, but he knew.

Kelsey shot Frankie a maddened look. "I found my heart! Okay?"

"Where was it?" He advanced on her with the sexiest smile she'd ever seen on his face. And she'd seen a number of his sexy smiles.

"With you," Kelsey snapped, wanting to step back, but her feet were not accommodating her.

Frankie looped his arms around her waist. "Now you know why I can't give you a divorce. I'm keeping your heart."

"Frankie." Kelsey's voice quivered.

"Yes?" He smiled into her face.

"Are you saying..." Kelsey floundered.

"That I love you?" He kissed the base of her neck. "Uh-huh."

Kelsey grabbed Frankie's shoulders, holding him for dear life. "But when..."

"When did I know?" He finished the question for her.

Kelsey nodded while Frankie drew her hair back with his fingers, wanting another look at her two earrings.

"I figured it out when you walked out the door with Eric, but I think deep inside I knew it way before then."

"But when I got back and told you that it was over with Eric, you pushed me away."

"I didn't think you felt the same about me as I felt about you." He set about showing her exactly how he felt with a long, possessive kiss.

There was a great big smile on Kelsey's well-kissed lips when he let go of her mouth. "Didn't you notice that I've been throwing myself at you?" she asked, shaking her head at him.

Frankie grinned and patted Kelsey's bottom. "Do you have any idea how hard I've had to fight not to jump all over you? You—" he pointed his finger at her "—have been driving me crazy."

The smile stayed on her face. "I didn't think you even wanted me anymore."

"I wanted the whole package, not just your body." His eyes turned suggestive. "I can tell you that right now I do have a few interesting thoughts about your body."

Kelsey gave him her sexiest look.

Frankie groaned. "We are going to have to get out of here. We've got some real honeymooning to do."

"Do you know what I wish?"

"What do you wish?" he asked, prepared to get her the moon.

"I wish that when we said our vows that we'd said them for real. It's going to always feel like our beginning was wrong. I didn't even say 'I do' the right way."

Frankie smiled tenderly. "Marry me again. We can do it right now."

"Now!" Kelsey exclaimed. "How can we get married right now?"

Frankie winked. "We've got a judge in the family and a wedding crowd right outside."

Frankie stood on the band platform with Judge Raymond DelGado and the bridal party. Teddy, Sonny, Shep and Johnny—at Lisa's pleading—were at his side. Quinn, Nancy, Angie and Lisa were opposite them.

The band had set up in a corner of the room. The singer, who had sung the blues through the evening, began the first refrain to Elvis Presley's "Love Me Tender," at Kelsey and Frankie's request.

Frankie gazed lovingly at Kelsey coming down the makeshift aisle he'd arranged. Her arm was linked through the arm of her grandfather. To Frankie, Kelsey couldn't have been more glowing if she'd been in a wedding gown and veil. She was carrying a bouquet of flowers that he'd somehow found the presence of mind to put together for her.

Kelsey smiled up at Frankie. Frankie took the steps down to the dance floor to accept her from her grandfather's arm.

Kelsey took Frankie's hand as Charlie let her go, but she halted. "Just a minute."

"Don't tell me we're going to have to discuss this?" Frankie grinned.

Kelsey shook her head, grinning back at him. "There's just something I have to do first."

Frankie watched Kelsey go after Charlie as he was making his way to his seat. When Kelsey embraced her grandfather, Frankie had to wipe away tears in his eyes. He walked to her, meeting her halfway. "Better?" he asked softly.

"Better," Kelsey answered in a lilting voice.

Frankie took Kelsey's hand and she linked her fingers with his. Together they made their way onto the platform.

Judge Raymond DelGado began. "We are gathered here together on this very special night for Kelsey and Frankie. In celebration, Kelsey and Frankie wish to consecrate their vows of matrimony for a second time now in the presence of family and friends."

There was a round of applause while Kelsey and Frankie smiled at each other.

The judge waved the crowd to silence. "Do you, Kelsey, take Frankie as your wedded husband, to have and to hold in sickness and in health, to love, to honor and to cherish until death do you part?"

"I do," Kelsey answered, facing Frankie with all the love she was feeling bright in her eyes while his eyes adored her.

"Do you, Frankie, take Kelsey as your wedded wife, to have and to hold in sickness and in health, to love, to honor and to cherish until death do you part?"

"I do," Frankie answered, the words coming from his heart and soul.

"Now in this time of reunion as we all offer you both our blessings, I ask that you keep in your minds the symbol of the rings you have already exchanged. So should your love remain—a circle without end.... And now, Frankie, you may kiss your wife."

Frankie found Kelsey's mouth this time ready and waiting for his. They kissed with exquisite joy, a reiteration of the vows they'd just taken, a sealing of hearts found and revered.

The band began to play and as they left the platform each thought of every tortured moment they were going to have to wait to be alone.

On their way out of the jazz club an hour later, Frankie said, "The first thing we're going to do when we get home is add your orange marmalade to our shopping list. I don't ever want to look at an almost empty jar again."

Kelsey's eyes began to fill with tears. Those words he'd just spoken were as poignant to her as their wedding vows. "What's the second thing we're going to do?"

Frankie winked sexily. "Do you have to ask?"

Kelsey's head moved from side to side, sending her two gold hoop earrings swinging.

* * * * *

MIRA™

The brightest star in women's fiction!

This October, reach for the stars and watch all your
dreams come true with **MIRA BOOKS**.

HEATHER GRAHAM POZZESSERE
Slow Burn in October
An enthralling tale of murder and passion set against
the dark and glittering world of Miami.

SANDRA BROWN
The Devil's Own in November
She made a deal with the devil...but she didn't bargain
on losing her heart.

BARBARA BRETTON
Tomorrow & Always in November
Unlikely lovers from very different worlds... They had to
cross time to find one another.

PENNY JORDAN
For Better For Worse in December
Three couples, three dreams—can they rekindle the love
and passion that first brought them together?

The sky has no limit with **MIRA BOOKS**.

HE'S MORE THAN A MAN, HE'S ONE OF OUR

Fabulous Fathers

DAD ON THE JOB
Linda Varner

Single dad Ethan Cooper didn't have time for women. But he needed Nicole Winter's business to get his new company going. Then he saw his latest client play mother to his two kids and he wanted her for so much more....

Dad on the Job is the first book in Linda Varner's **MR. RIGHT, INC.**, a heartwarming new series about three hardworking bachelors in the building trade who find love at first sight—construction site, that is! Beginning in October.

Fall in love with our Fabulous Fathers!

Silhouette
R O M A N C E™

FF1094

Premiere

The stars are out in October at Silhouette! Read
captivating love stories by talented *new* authors—
in their very first Silhouette appearance.

Sizzle with Susan Crosby's
THE MATING GAME—Desire #888
...when Iain Mackenzie and Kani Warner are forced
to spend their days—and *nights*—together in *very* close
tropical quarters!

Explore the passion in Sandra Moore's
HIGH COUNTRY COWBOY—Special Edition #918
...where Jake Valiteros tries to control the demons that
haunt him—along with a stubborn woman as wild as the
Wyoming wind.

Cherish the emotion in Kia Cochrane's
MARRIED BY A THREAD—Intimate Moments #600
...as Dusty McKay tries to recapture the love he once
shared with his wife, Tori.

Exhilarate in the power of Christie Clark's
TWO HEARTS TOO LATE—Romance #1041
...as Kirby Anne Gordon and Carl Tannon fight for custody
of a small child...and battle their growing attraction!

Shiver with Val Daniels'
BETWEEN DUSK AND DAWN—Shadows #42
...when a mysterious stranger claims to want to save
Jonna Sanders from a serial killer.

Catch the classics of tomorrow—*premiering* today—
Only from

Silhouette®

TM

PREM94

Jilted!

Left at the altar, but not for long.

Why are these six couples
who have sworn off love
suddenly hearing wedding bells?

Find out in these scintillating books
by your favorite authors,
coming this November!

#889 **THE ACCIDENTAL BRIDEGROOM**
by Ann Major
(Man of the Month)

#890 **TWO HEARTS, SLIGHTLY USED**
by Dixie Browning

#891 **THE BRIDE SAYS NO**
by Cait London

#892 **SORRY, THE BRIDE HAS ESCAPED**
by Raye Morgan

#893 **A GROOM FOR RED RIDING HOOD**
by Jennifer Greene

#894 **BRIDAL BLUES**
by Cathie Linz

Come join the festivities when six handsome
hunks finally walk down the aisle...

only from

SILHOUETTE® Desire®

JILT

SILHOUETTE®
Desire®

ANNETTE BROADRICK'S
SONS OF TEXAS
SERIES CONTINUES

Available in October from Silhouette Desire, TEMPTATION TEXAS STYLE! (SD #883) is the latest addition to Annette Broadrick's series about the Callaway family.

Roughed-up rodeo cowboy Tony Callaway thought women were nothing but trouble—but once this lonesome cowboy took one look into Christina O'Reilly's sultry green eyes, he was sure to change his mind!

Don't miss Tony Callaway's story in TEMPTATION TEXAS STYLE! by Annette Broadrick, Desire's MAN OF THE MONTH for October.

**He's one of the SONS OF TEXAS and
ready to ride into your heart!**

SDAB